Chancing It

Matthew Yorke

WAYWISER

First published in 2005 by

THE WAYWISER PRESS

9 Woodstock Road, London N4 3ET, UK
P.O. Box 6205, Baltimore, MD 21206, USA
www.waywiser-press.com

Editor
Philip Hoy

Editorial Advisors
Joseph Harrison   Clive Watkins   Greg Williamson

Copyright © Matthew Yorke, 2005

The right of Matthew Yorke to be identified as the author of this work
has been asserted by him in accordance with the
Copyright, Designs and Patents Act of 1988.

All rights reserved

A CIP catalogue record for this book is available from the British Library

ISBN-10: 1-904130-18-6

ISBN-13: 978-1-904130-18-5

Printed and bound by
Cromwell Press Ltd., Trowbridge, Wiltshire

To Euan

ONE

"Right, *toolbox talk* ... Gather round everybody. That's it: fan out, grab a chair. Good morning everyone. First, a very warm welcome to the two new faces here this morning. They are Steve Marsden and Helena Wright. Welcome to *The Pennine Recycling Plant.* Could you please stand up both of you? Steve and Helena are here on work experience from Wentworth High School. They'll be with us for a fortnight and I hope that come Friday week they'll have formed an idea of how our service benefits the community. And understand how a small recycling plant like *Pennine* – if this were replicated in all the towns and villages world-wide – how this could make a real difference to the future of the planet. Thank you: you can sit down now."

Steve had been staring at his trainers. He was shy by nature. As he sank to his chair he glanced at Helena. In contrast she was smiling, looking around at the fifteen workers and volunteers, quite unabashed.

"Every morning, Steve and Helena, we have what we call a *toolbox talk.* This helps us to focus on our objective in a collective fashion. That way we become more than the sum of our parts – isn't that right, everybody?"

General nodding.

"It's also a time and a place in which we can air any grievances and concerns about working practices, remembering to put safety first in all instances. Because we want this facility to be efficient and a place which respects all workers as human beings. That way our productivity begins to sing – like a songbird, as I have sometimes been known to say."

When Steve had come for the interview in May, he had thought this guy – Robin Fellowes was his name – was a bit of a headcase. Today he was wearing the same lumberjack shirt, the same black-rimmed spectacles, and his hair, barely long enough to warrant it, was bunched and tied in a sprouting ponytail at the back of his collar.

Once more Steve glanced at Helena. Again she was smiling, in fact she was beaming in Robin's direction as if to say: I can't wait to get started.

"So, first off: working practices. Any comments anyone?"

"People still aren't putting their tools away," someone said.

"I'm glad you brought that up. Tools must be returned to their rightful positions." Robin waved behind his back where the profiles of screwdrivers, wrenches and hammers had been outlined on the walls with magic marker. "Otherwise time is lost in searching for them, and lost time means what?"

Steve was amazed to see Helena raise her hand.

"Yes, Helena?"

"Lost time means lost productivity!" she answered.

"It means exactly that," Robin deliberately nodded in approval. "I can see that Helena is going to fit in very well at *Pennine Recycling*."

Steve frowned. If truth were told, he had written to *The Pennine Recycling Plant* asking them for a fortnight's work experience only on the strength of Helena's successful application. He had initially contacted the local football club – to no avail. He had then tried *Hotel 413* in town, where celebrities – DJs, pop stars and performers – were known to stay when passing through on their tours (it was even rumoured that Nelson Mandela had spent the night here on his visit to West Yorkshire in 2001). And had come up against a brick wall. At one point his stepfather, Martin, had tried to rope him into working with him in property maintenance – but this would be a very last resort. Finally it had dawned on him to follow his heart!

Robin was winding up now. "I think that's it for this morning. It only remains for us to gather our thoughts."

Steve looked on in horror as the fifteen workers began to rise to their feet and hold hands. He found he had no option but to join in, as the two men either side were quick to proffer hot, sweaty, outstretched fingers. Steve saw most of the workers close their eyes and raise their chins. These people could have been in church.

"The thought for today," Robin began when everyone was ready; *The longest journey begins with the first step."* He paused before finishing: "We shall go on stepping until our journey is done, until our goal is attained: forward we march."

"Forward we march," some repeated under their breaths.

Steve and Helena, being young workers, were placed directly under Robin's guidance and control. As they moved about the hangar-type building he gave them a potted history of the facility. Not long established, there were at present only three sections within *The Pennine Recycling Plant*: fridges, cookers and hoovers. The general premise was that any fridge, cooker or hoover collected off the streets by the council or found dumped at the waste depot on Low Road would be assessed with a view to reconditioning. If the appliance looked as if it still had some potential, it would be given a complete overhaul by qualified technicians, subjected to all the necessary safety tests, then either sold cheap or given to a deserving family.

It was amazing what people threw away, Robin told them. Sometimes it was just a question of a fuse on a hoover; other times it was the seal on the fridge door that needed replacing. An hour's work and that item was back in circulation, benefiting someone in the community; but also, perhaps more importantly, denying the producer the opportunity to make another unit to fill the void. In point of fact it was not only a question of people being ignorant about fuses and the mechanics of appliances: it was also that people had gone consumer mad. The big companies and corporations, driven by anonymous shareholders and their greed for profits, instil the idea in people that fridges, cookers and hoovers must be changed every two years. This was quickly becoming what Robin liked to call an "add to basket society". Just one click on an icon was all that it took these days. But that was another subject ...

At tea break Steve sat next to Helena.

"The man's a lunatic," he whispered.

"Do you think so?"

"Don't you?"

"I think he speaks a lot of sense."

"Bit crazy all that holding hands stuff ..."

"If that's what it takes."

"If you ask me you can change a plug without chanting a load of mumbo jumbo first."

At eleven o'clock they began in earnest. Robin gave them both latex gloves as there were sometimes some "sharp edges", as he called them. Together they took the backs off three full sized fridges, first removing all the posidrive screws, then gently easing the covers off with a miniature tommy bar.

"There's not much point in cleaning them all out inside until we've made an assessment of the motor and electrics," Robin explained. "Now these backs are off we give them a good vacuum and have a proper look: see what's what."

With a hand-sized vacuum cleaner Robin demonstrated what he expected of his young charges, and then left them to it. The wiring had attracted dust in the same way as a magnet attracts iron filings. It was rewarding work, seeing the years of dirt disappear into the powerful hose. Before long the circuitry of all three fridges was spotless. Robin nodded in approval.

"Now we give them what's called a PAT: a portable appliance

test," he said, "and if they pass that and the general condition doesn't seem too bad inside, then we're in business."

"Call this business?" Steve whispered to Helena as Robin knelt out of earshot.

"Why are you always so negative?" she asked, turning and frowning, and her expression told him that he should tread carefully.

In silence they watched the PAT being carried out.

"Yes, yes and yes," Robin said at length, standing and clapping his hands. "Excellent work. These three fridges could be back in circulation by the end of the month." He seemed quite animated now. "Just imagine it: instead of rotting away in a rubbish dump, they will actually be doing what they're designed to do: keep things cool."

There was a strict procedure to follow now. They had to write down the serial number on a special form, along with the model and manufacturer's name. Then a description of the general condition of the fridge from the ice box to the salad box, indicating if they thought any doors or trays were missing. Finally it was cleaning time. Robin gave them both tabards.

"Put that on; it will save your clothes."

Steve was loath to obey; but as he saw the grease and dirt within the fridges turn the foaming detergent black almost immediately, he relented: for whatever reason – in fact he knew the reason perfectly well – he had put on his best jeans and a new Nike top that morning.

ॐ

Steve was at home in the kitchen. Mary-Anne, his mother, was next door in the front living room, with Martin, her husband of eight years. Martin would be lying on the sofa – you could bet money on it. Steve could picture his exact position, a hand half supporting his head, his feet castellated on the armrest. Mary-Anne must be ironing since, over the sound of the television, he could just hear the iron being placed on its end each time his mother rearranged the material over the board and the occasional whisper of evaporating water on hot metal. Then there were footsteps over the bare floorboards.

"I spend my whole life opening windows in this house," he heard her say.

"And I spend my whole life closing them," Martin replied.

"Do you want to live in an airless oven?"

"Do you want to share your life with a thousand flies?"

The ironing was resumed.

"Is that you for the evening?" Mary-Anne then asked.

"What do you mean?"

"Lying there like you haven't seen a bed in four months."

"Oh, so you've been excavating drains all day, have you? Pardon me for not noticing."

"Martin, if you're that tired you should take some vitamins," Steve heard his mother finish in a more serious tone.

"Vitamins, my arse."

Steve's father, Edmund Marsden, had been knocked down and killed by joy-riders as he crossed Bell Lane in 1992. Steve had been three years old. He had dim memories of that afternoon: the activity, the coming and going of friends and family. But he had been too young to comprehend and absorb what had really happened. He could remember telling a friend at school "My daddy's in the ground", and crying – but there had been little pain. What had happened was a fact of life. These days he found there was a void, an emptiness within him; but still no pain as such. There were some things that made him lonely though. Like the sound of traffic. As the crow flies, they lived a mile from the motorway, and on a still night you could hear the grind of gears and throbbing of engines as the juggernauts laboured under their loads. Sometimes that noise "took you with it", and Steve used to think it could lead him to his father. That reverberation through the night air still had the power to make him feel sad and alone.

His eyes fell to the table where Martin had thrown his papers and lunchbox on returning from work. There was a *Daily Mirror* and a sheaf of estate agent's particulars. The *Mirror* was folded open on the sports page, more particularly on the racing cards – Martin liked a flutter. The top of the page was scrolled with doodles and beside the names of a handful of horses he had made deliberate marks with the point of his biro. One horse, *The Twitcher* running in the 3.30 at Sandown, was heavily underscored.

The estate agent's particulars were of more interest. "An outstanding investment opportunity in an-up and-coming area'" one boasted in dark print below a picture of a semi-detached property. Or: "A rare opportunity to acquire a superb pied-a-terre with porterage and dedicated car port". The property market had been a prevalent topic of conversation in the house of late. Indeed that was exactly what Martin and Mary-Anne were discussing now.

"I just don't want to leave it too late," he heard Martin say. "There are some cracking properties out there."

"The bubble's got to burst some time," his mother objected.

"That's what they've been saying for the last three years. And what have we seen? A thirty percent increase year in, year out."

"That's not to say the market isn't going to collapse when we get into it."

"And that's not to say we might get run down by a bus tomorrow morning."

"Martin, don't!"

"Sorry: that was thoughtless. But Mary-Anne ..."

Steve could hear Martin change position: sit up or stand.

"We must do something," he implored.

"Must we? Haven't we got enough as it is?"

"I don't know ... I just feel I need a bit more of a *challenge* in life. You're always telling me to get off my backside. Well: to buy a property, do it up and sell it on a rising market – what could be more rewarding than that? That would put a smile on all of our faces each morning."

"You're right, I know," Steve heard his mother sigh. "It just seems a risk. I'm not a gambler by nature – like you."

"I'm not a gambler. My horses are just a bit of fun."

It was strange, but when you eavesdropped discussions or conversations you were somehow cognisant of the real facts better than if you were there in the room, face to face with the talkers. Perhaps all the facial mannerisms and hand gestures went some way to disguising the truth. Of course the horses *were* a bit of fun for Martin; but they could also become an unhealthy interest at times, almost verging on the obsessive. Mary-Anne knew this as well as anyone, yet she said: "I know, love. And you must have your fun."

"So shall we talk to the bank?" Martin persevered.

"I suppose so."

The purpose behind talking to the bank was no secret: Steve had been privy to the reasoning and ramifications on many occasions. The fact was that Martin had worked hard to build up a reputation in his line of work, but – like many others in his position and not withstanding the fact that property development was on the up – he found that he was not always in work: there were slack moments. Moreover a better part of his money was paid in cash, not passing through what Martin referred to as "the books". The end result was that his income on paper was relatively small. To buy a property to develop he would need to borrow from the bank. And with the bank lending only three-and-a-half times a person's income – there wasn't going to be enough, not nearly.

Mary-Anne was in a similar predicament. It wasn't through any failure of book-keeping; she was scrupulous in her accounts. But being a typist working from home she had seen the volume of work decrease steadily over the past ten years. The advent of personal computers had put paid to her once quite lucrative trade. There were still three authors who always engaged her to type their manuscripts from longhand; and there were half a dozen local businesses which employed her part-time, dropping off audiocassettes from which to type up articles and letters. But there was no getting away from it: her income was not as great or as reliable as it had once been.

The only way to raise enough money to purchase an investment property would be to borrow against this house, No. 14 Stanningley Terrace. It would not be easy, given the substance of their affairs, but the house was owned outright and was a valuable asset.

"What do you think it's worth?" Steve heard Martin ask of his mother.

"You'd know better than me."

"I would say two hundred thousand."

"Two hundred thousand?"

"And rising ..."

"I doubt it somehow."

"There's only one way to find out. Let's get it valued on Monday."

"Are you sure, Martin?"

"Won't cost us a penny. Nothing ventured, nothing gained."

"I'll have to hoover first."

There was something about these speculations which pained Steve. He had heard talk of buying, selling, mortgaging, on a number of occasions, and it had been freely acknowledged that without this house there would be no future in any dreams of this kind. The tender part was that this house was a legacy of his father's. The joy-riders had had no insurance, of course; but Edmund Marsden had been a shrewd man: he had insured his life against this shocking eventuality, so that his family – Mary-Anne and their two sons, Vincent and Steven – would find themselves at least with a roof over their heads. Any speculating with this "provision" was in some manner tampering with his will or his good intentions. Steve rose and entered the sitting room. He did this really to pre-empt any further elaboration on the matter.

"Steve, hi," his mother greeted him.

"Hi."

"How's the second-hand shop?" Martin goaded.

"It's not a second-hand shop. It's a recycling plant."

"I know that: but how is it?"

"The boss needs therapy."

"Steven ..."

"He needs a reality check, big style – he does."

"Whenever I open the local paper I see a picture of Robin Fellowes," his mother said. "You mark my words: that man knows what he's doing."

"He had us holding hands," Steve complained.

"If that's what it takes ..."

Steve grunted. Weren't those exactly Helena's words?

"Are you staying in now?" Mary-Anne asked.

"I'm going to meet Buzz in a minute."

"Where's Buzz working then?" Martin asked.

"At *Kwik-Fit*."

"Jesus wept ..."

TWO

It was four days on, and Robin, Steve, Helena and two others were sitting outside *Pennine Recycling* on some deck chairs that they had found on one of their trips to the tip on Low Road. It was lunch break.

Steve was sitting opposite Helena, the sun on his shoulders. She, with the rays full in her face, sat well back, eyelids closed against the brightness. Placed in this manner, Steve could study her without fear of being seen. Her hair was up in two bunches today and the sun glistened on her marble-white teeth, just visible. She wore the same pair of dungarees as always; only her top was different: a short-sleeved, lilac T-shirt. Her feet were petite, the instep well-defined like an eyebrow in caricature. The day before, she had painted her toenails a deep, deep cherry crimson. To Steve's eyes she was far and away the sexiest girl in his year; yet if she knew this she certainly didn't flaunt it.

"At the end of the day," Robin was saying, "it's the man in the street who's going to have the last say. People the world over have learnt to vote with their feet. Look at the fall of communism in Russia and in places like Poland. Steve and Helena, you're probably too young to remember this, but the people just said: enough is enough; we can't go on like this. And in a great act of bravery, borne out of despair and frustration, they stood up to the tanks and dictators."

He paused before continuing.

"And that's what is beginning to happen to the big corporations. People are saying: the planet will not survive at this rate, we've got to change the way we do things. But the beauty of it is, no one has got to stand in front of a tank this time – they just have to invest their money in companies that have a social and environmental conscience. By putting their money in companies that are going to act responsibly they effectively have some say in what goes on. And that's what we're after, because at the rate things have been going the situation could easily spiral out of control."

Steve was watching Helena as he asked of Robin: "You don't agree with the rioting at those global demonstrations, then?" And was pleased to see her open her eyes in anticipation of the response.

"I don't believe in violence," Robin said deliberately. "I was at that rally in London. The movement lost a lot of credibility that afternoon. Changes must come about by peaceful means."

"Freedom fighters aren't always peaceful though, are they?" Steve objected.

"No, they aren't; that's quite correct. But I believe this battle for the planet can be waged and won by peaceful means. I really do."

"I hope you're right," Steve nodded. He had said this as a teacher might speak to a pupil, the words ringing with a patronising edge. It sounded cheeky coming from Steve, and he saw Robin sit up a little. He also saw Helena's top lip lift in a half-grin. She had a sense of humour then!

"But," Robin rose abruptly from his chair, "actions speak louder than words. Come on: forward we march."

It was incredible the way some people lived their lives. There was one fridge that Steve was given – probably as a reward for his impertinence – which was beyond the pale, shockingly filthy. ("Definitely worth saving, that one," Robin had said. "It's a British make.") But if Steve had had his way he would have sent it straight back to the dump. As soon as you opened the door a rank smell of mildew and rotting food hit you between the eyes, and whoever had owned it had managed to break some eggs in the scalloped egg compartment. The yolks, bearded with mould, had glued the shattered shells to the plastic. And what was worse, the organic, environmentally friendly detergent which Robin had proudly issued to them, was quite simply not up to the job. They had to work doubly hard. Was this really how you saved the planet?

Just before tea, however, there was an opportunity for Steve to shine.

"Oh my God, oh my God," he heard one of the part-time girls scream at the far end of the workshop. Several other workers rushed to her side, forming a tight knot in front of the bench.

"Stand back everyone," Robin commanded. "Let me through. What seems to be the problem?"

"How sick can you get?" another murmured with disgust, stepping back.

"Oh my God; oh my God."

Then there was silence.

"I can't make that out at all," Robin eventually pronounced.

"We should find out where this fridge came from and report them to the RSPCA."

"There must be an explanation."

"A cruel, sick mind ..."

Steve and Helena made their way towards the commotion. Craning their necks, they peered in the general direction of the focus of attention, which appeared to be the icebox of a Zanussi fridge. One of the male volunteers was holding open the hinged door with a screwdriver, his lips contorted in disgust. There seemed to be what looked like a Tupperware container inside. Through the frosted plastic they could make out the outline of a dead animal, or maybe a tangle of dead animals, with areas of white and grey fur combined with pink skin, tails or feet.

"I can't make it out at all," Robin repeatedly murmured. The fact that he could not offer a logical explanation seemed to be of growing concern to him.

Steve stepped forward, ten pairs of eyes on him. "I know what that is."

"Really?"

"They're fuzzies."

"Fuzzies?"

"Mice. The owner of that fridge kept snakes. That's snake food."

"He's right, you know," the man with the screwdriver declared, and all assembled nodded gravely in agreement. Of course: it was obvious now. The crowd began to dissolve, nervous laughter dissipating the once tense atmosphere within the workshop.

"We might have spent hours puzzling that one out," Robin congratulated Steve. "Not so much as a snake in the grass but a snake in the fridge! What?"

There was a particular odour in Greenglades Home for the Elderly. It greeted you as soon as the automatic door silently retracted to beckon you over the threshold. Mrs Holland had often jokingly remarked on it: was it *Alpine Freshness* or *Ozone Haze*? In her room, however, there were always cut flowers on the table beside the window. These she ordered by telephone from *Interflora*: "My one luxury", as she called it with an expression of feigned guilt.

"Where's your brother?" Mrs Holland asked. Her voice was soft, her words well rounded.

Steve was sitting on the plastic-covered armchair on the right hand side of the bed. "Vinnie's in Amsterdam," he replied.

"My: in Amsterdam," Mrs Holland cooed. "What's he doing there?"

"He's gone with a bunch of friends."

Mrs Holland nodded wisely. It was no secret that Vinnie was going through a difficult phase (smoking weed, hanging out with the "wrong" crowd); Mary-Anne herself had probably discussed the situation with Mrs Holland during one of her own visits. Which was only natural, because, if it was advice you wanted or the opportunity to get something off your chest, there was no better place to come. The old lady's reflections were not only sound, wrought from years of experience and acquired insights, but more importantly you could tell Mrs Holland anything without fear of being judged. She took things at face value: there was a cause and effect in the workings of the world.

"I hope he's being careful," was all she offered.

There was a brief silence, broken by the sound of a trolley being pushed down the corridor outside.

"And you're working at the *Recycling Plant*, I hear?"

"Just for a fortnight."

"Good for you," Mrs Holland nodded thoughtfully. "Are you enjoying it?"

"Sort of."

"I think I'm ready for recycling," the old lady then said with a mischievous look.

"Mrs Holland!"

"Well, I am, aren't I? And so what? I've had a lovely life, filled to the brim. And I don't fear death. Not in the least bit. What's that expression: *death, where is thy sting?*"

"You'll live till you're a hundred," Steve replied (these were the exact words his mother had used on the occasion of Mrs Holland's eightieth birthday).

Mrs Holland looked suddenly serious; there was almost a note of reproach in her voice. "I don't want to live till I'm a hundred! If I could be of some use, then maybe. But sitting here ... watching the cricket ..." She laughed her rich, warm laugh. "England were all out for two hundred and fourteen at lunch."

"I know," Steve looked up, at once more animated. "They can't seem to get the measure of that new bowler."

Sometimes when Steve came on his weekly visits to see Mrs Holland at this home they sat in silence for the full thirty minutes. Yet still he invariably felt refreshed and rewarded by their time together. Not rewarded in a selfish way, as some people might feel when giving to charity, but rewarded for what she had given to him. Having been a companion of his grandmother, Florence Marsden, in the 1970s, she was the only remaining link with a past long gone. For this reason he felt that she understood him like no other. Mrs Holland also had an uncanny knack of reading minds.

"Your father used to love his cricket, too," she said.

Steve reddened.

"Do you think of him often?" Mrs Holland asked.

"Quite often."

"He would be so proud of you, I know. So proud of both of you."

It seemed only right for Steve to say: "I like Martin though."

Mrs Holland always came straight to the point. "But it's not the same, is it? And Martin knows that."

They sat in silence for some minutes. Steve watched a blackbird ferreting for worms on the lawn outside. It would hop, listen, hop and then strike, its plumage a lustrous black against the short-cropped grass. He was pleased to see it climb to an oak by the roadside with a worm swinging from its beak.

"What happened to your father … seemed … so *senseless*," Mrs Holland tried to articulate, her eyes peering as if into the middle distance. "There was no reason to it. No earthly reason. But who are we to judge?"

"Mum and Martin are getting the house valued," Steve suddenly volunteered, as if he unconsciously wished to check this line of conversation.

Mrs Holland came out of her reverie with a jolt. "Mary-Anne's selling?" she asked with real interest.

"Not selling, but perhaps using it as … what's it called? … collateral to buy another property."

"Another property?"

"One for Martin to do up."

"I do hope they're careful," was once again Mrs Holland's pronouncement. "But they'll know much better than me about that sort of thing."

A nurse knocked quietly and entered. "Would you like a shower this evening, Mrs Holland?" she asked.

"Is it that time already?"

Steve rose to his feet. "I should be making tracks," he said.

"Before you go, Steven: I was wondering if you could come on Sunday ... with Vinnie. I need to see you both together about something."

"Yes, of course," he replied, surprised at the request.

"Only if it's convenient, mind."

"We'll be here on Sunday, same time."

~

Steve had arranged to meet Buzz at the bandstand. He found him instead in front of the park gates, staring through the driver's window of a BMW five series, new model. Buzz barely looked up as Steve approached.

"Will you look at that?" he whispered eventually. "This is the ultimate."

"It's just a car, Buzz!"

"Steven, my friend, there are *cars* and there are *cars*."

"And this is a car!"

"Yes – a car that cost forty grand plus ... You can almost smell what it cost!"

"Does that make it any more of a car?"

There was an edge of irony in Buzz's voice. "In this car I could be *someone*."

"Someone who's not you, you mean?"

They made their way into the park proper. The evening – it was in fact after nine p.m. – was warm and sultry; yet a faint suspicion of damp warned of the approaching night.

"Is that Anita and Mel?" Buzz asked, staring into the gloaming.

" ... Your Anita."

"Watch it!"

It was indeed Anita and Mel. Both were perched on the railings of one side of the bandstand's hexagon, as if riding side-saddle. Anita wore pink: pink pedal pushers ruched at the knee, a pink boob tube and string vest to match. Mel wore her usual black: she was a part-time Goth or a Goth in-the-making. No one could quite make her out. All four acknowledged each other with casual, barely audible grunts.

"Work experience going okay, then?" Anita asked of Steve.

"Not bad. And yours?"

"Can't complain. Helena with you, is she?"

"She's there."

"That's not what I asked."

"Then I don't understand your question."

It was no secret that Anita held a candle for Steve. But it was one way traffic. Sometimes Steve would ask himself why the feelings were not reciprocated, since Anita was a girl who had won the hearts of many of his peers. In his quest for an answer he would lazily fantasise about her, tasting the freshness of her warm breath, feeling the texture of her satin-smooth skin, tracing the stepping stones of the vertebrae on the back of her neck, these aglow with tiny blond hairs – yet he always came to the same conclusion: he simply did not fancy her. Certainly, if they were to embrace, he would forget himself; but as they untangled themselves, his sense of their separateness would instantly be restored to him. It was Helena, not Anita, who interested him.

"Where are you then?" Steve asked of them both.

"*Body Shop*, can't you tell?" Mel answered and both collapsed in gales of laughter.

"I phoned in sick at *Kwik-Fit* this morning," Buzz volunteered. "I'm selling them trackers with my dad; we're going to make some brass, you know. It's serious this time."

"We've heard that one before," Anita mocked.

"Well, I earned fifty quid today, and that was just before lunch."

"Believe *that* when I see it."

"See it then," and Buzz withdrew a neat wad of notes held tightly together with a silver clasp.

"He has and all," Mel murmured.

Steve had heard Buzz speak of these trackers before. Once fitted to delivery vans and the cars of salesmen the idea was that the boss could monitor the whereabouts of the company's vehicles to the nearest postcode and the exact moment in time. It worked by satellite apparently. The beam would get bounced up to a number of receptors. The information was then calculated by means of trigonometry. There was a growing demand for these devices since – according to Buzz's father – there were a lot of "skivers" around, a lot of employees these days who, given half a chance, would "toss it off".

But Buzz's father was a lot of hot air and basically quite an unpleasant man. On their way to bowling one Saturday afternoon Steve had been shocked to hear him boasting to another parent of his other part-time job as a bailiff (his main job was working as a taxi driver). "It's the poor people who pay quickest," he had said, "and the richer lot in their big houses who think they can string you along ... because they think that you're just a little man in a car. But they're very much mistaken, *very* much mistaken. I say: you've had your day in court; I'm quite in my rights to kick your door down; now pay up." If he, Steve, owed money, Buzz's father would be the last person on earth he would want to see on his doorstep. The man had no scruples whatsoever – the type who, given the slightest provocation, would lamp you. Indeed, only last term Buzz had come to school one morning with a bruised cheek.

"So what do you do then with the trackers? Pack them?" Anita asked with a dismissive laugh.

"I sell them."

"Do you chuff ..."

"Arrange appointments, that's all. *'Hello, good morning, my name's Ben Fairclough from a company called* Precision Trackers ... *To whom am I speaking, please? ... Ahh, good morning to you, Anita. May I just take two minutes of your time to introduce myself and the company?'*" There was a winning ring to Buzz's voice. He spoke his words slower and deeper than he would normally. If you were the other end of a telephone you would believe yourself to be talking to an adult, not a teenager. Anita looked impressed now.

"*'We lease and fit satellite-tracking systems to fleet vehicles. You've probably read about this exciting new technology which can pinpoint a vehicle's position to within thirty metres, and provide printouts of all visits, drops, etc., etc. We have a sales representative in your area on Friday morning: I was wondering if we could arrange a brief appointment to establish whether our equipment could be of any use to your company?'* And if you get an appointment and the rep gets in through the door: fifteen pounds. Doesn't matter whether they make a sale or not. It's called leads."

"And do you get commission as well?" Mel asked.

"For every tracker fitted, you get thirty-five pounds. If it were a company with a fleet of ten vans you'd be looking at three hundred and fifty. Then sell more than five hundred pounds' worth of business in a week and you get a bonus."

"Better than selling soap," Mel grunted.

"Or recycling fridges," Buzz added.

"Don't knock the fridges," Steve laughed. "It's not everyday that you get to do something for the environment."

All four were united in laughter.

THREE

Steve was sitting in Vinnie's bedroom. The curtains were still partially drawn. It was overcast outside and a grey, thin light diffused the area between the brothers. A half-unpacked holdall lay on the floor, the unzipped sides hanging loosely open. In this gloom it resembled a clam on the ocean bed, the dark recess within the case perhaps promising bait for an unsuspecting prey. Whether he wore an iPod or sat listening to his stereo Vinnie was always surrounded by music. Now a strain of Acid Jazz, its walking bass line strident like a heartbeat, filled the air.

"He's going to become a property developer?" Vinnie repeated.

"That's what he is now, isn't he?"

"He's a builder," Vinnie bluntly pronounced. "And Mum's okay with the idea of him going into *business*?"

"As far as I can make out."

The older brother shrugged. "Whatever makes them happy."

Vinnie was fiddling with his iPod. The fact that fifteen hundred songs could be stored on this, an object no bigger than a packet of crayons, would never cease to impress Steve. He would ask for one of these for his next birthday, he thought, knowing full well that the request would be turned down on grounds of expense. Vinnie had bought this iPod with his own money.

"What was Amsterdam like?" he asked.

"Okay."

"Just okay?"

"It was cool actually."

"What did you do?"

"Chilled out in the coffee shops. Hung around the red-light district ..."

"Smoke a lot of weed?"

"Yeah, plenty. Why, you want some?" And Vinnie pulled a transparent packet from his trouser pocket. Inside was a lump of black, resinous hash, so sticky that it had welded itself to the plastic, producing opaque air traps.

"God, Vinnie ... How much did you bring back?"

Vinnie's answer was designed to produce as much embarrassment as possible. "You really don't *ask* that sort of question," he drawled.

A silence came between them. Steve had no interest in marijuana. On the occasions he had experimented with it (with Buzz in fact) it had made him uncannily nervous – "paras" as he was informed it was known. It was as if he were walking on a frozen lake, the ice throwing out cracks ahead of his tentative feet, all the while a sound like a high tensile fence being knocked with a stick ringing in his ears. At any moment he would be submerged in freezing water, a ceiling of unbreakable ice above his head. "You've got to go with the flow," Buzz had explained. It was to no avail. Then once the nerves had abated, almost as if driven away by exhaustion, a lethargy like no other he had experienced set in. He had been like an insect caught in honey: to sit up was an exercise in itself, an effort that had brought stars to the periphery of his vision. Finally there had been the gratifying realisation that he had "done" that now and, if he so wished, he need never do it again.

"Mrs Holland has asked us to go in to to see her," Steve remembered.

"Why?"

"I'm not sure. She said she wanted to see us both together about something. Sunday, yeah?"

"Okay."

Steve stood. "And Mum wants us out when the surveyor gets

here."

Vinnie shrugged. "Going out anyway," he shrugged.

"Coming back later?"

"Dunno," the older boy answered. "Got to see a man about a dog."

～

On a morning like this you could see the Emley Moor Television Mast from miles and miles around. You might be travelling south on the M1, in which case it would be on your right; you might be between Huddersfield and Halifax; in that case it would be to the West. It was said that on an exceptionally clear day you could even see it from Beverley.

His class had done a project on the mast only that spring. 1,084 feet tall, taller than the Eiffel Tower in Paris; 24,000 tonnes total weight; eighty foot diameter girth at its base. Icicles falling from the structure had threatened the village of Emley, and they had planned to build a canopy to protect the houses and the Methodist Chapel. But the storm of 1969 had beaten them to it. The mast collapsed and lay broken on the moor, like Goliath slain. The structure had been "under-engineered" as the science teacher put it: the bending moment had been incorrectly calculated. It took an American firm to build it right. "That was the beginning of the end," the teacher had said one afternoon in a deliberate, sad tone.

It was not the end, however. This town, encircled by moor, heather on the higher slopes, windswept grass on the lower reaches, still remained a thrumming hive of activity. Walking into town, the steep bank falling to the road on the right contained by a dyke of blackened sandstone centuries old, the valley to your left deep yet unmenacing, you could feel on top of the world. Of course some of the older industries had gone, but others had taken their place. People berated the banks and service industries, but a job was a job, surely? And wasn't it preferable to be working in an air-conditioned office than in a mill smelting iron? People always went on about the death of manufacturing. But you couldn't have it both ways.

The plan was to meet Buzz in Queen's Court. Steve saw that he was twenty-five minutes early, however. So at the bottom of Town Street he turned left. A new Italian Restaurant, San Petino, had opened here, and the green, white and red facade had excited his curiosity some days before. He would sit on a bench opposite and watch the world go by.

This place was indeed the talk of the town. In just a few minutes a procession of expensive-looking vehicles stopped, allowed their passengers to disembark, then set off again to park around the block. A few minutes later the drivers of these vehicles would reappear, straightening their ties, patting their wallet pockets as they passed, businesslike, over the threshold.

A man selling *The Big Issue* drew Steve's attention. By his familiar air with the clientele of this restaurant you might have mistaken him for a doorman engaged by the management. For each car that parked momentarily before the entrance received the same treatment: hand gestures to bring the passenger door adjacent to the flagged entrance lined with planters; further hand-gestures directing drivers not in the know to the best places to park; a welcoming nod for each so theatrical it almost verged on a bow. And all this accomplished with a warm, toothless smile. He held a clear plastic bag containing his copies of *The Big Issue* close to his stomach – only it became apparent when one lady pointed to the magazine that there was in reality only one copy inside that bag. He might have been a vendor on other days, but today he was a beggar.

Steve watched with growing interest. It seemed that one in every three of four people to approach the restaurant's glass doors gave the man a coin. And, judging by the way the coin was held, deliberately between thumb and forefinger, it was a one-pound coin. There seemed no difference as regards sex: men and women tipped equally. Some went out of their way to donate money, holding back until the rest of their party had entered, exchanging a few words with the vendor, almost enacting a play out of their show of generosity. Others gave as if unconsciously or out of habit.

In the ten minutes Steve was sitting opposite San Petino, he saw money change hands over a dozen times. If things continued in this vein there would be good reason for the waiters of that establishment to feel envy and resentment, he reflected. Then the atmosphere abruptly changed, or – to be more accurate – it was the vendor's manner and expression that suddenly altered. The smile was gone: now he looked hunted, haunted. Steve glanced about to see what had warranted this: it was the approach of two men, one ginger-haired, the other dark.

The fairer man stood some five paces off, idly pushing at a chain that hung between concrete bollards with the sole of his shoe. It was the darker man, short though stocky, who advanced to the vendor. An exchange ensued. To a passer-by it would appear that the darker man was the more reasonable of the two: he gestured deliberately with both hands, palms turned skywards. Whatever it was that was being discussed was, from his point of view, a *fait accompli*. The vendor by contrast gesticulated wildly. "No, no," Steve could see him articulate. "No way." Finally, after an act that had the vendor retreating down the sidewalk as if to say "Enough is enough", a compromise was made and he half turned away to count an agreed amount from a fistful of coins. The sum of money was then handed over. And all the while, the fairer man looked on, disinterested, bored. A minute later they were both gone.

Steve saw the vendor walk some paces off and turn once more as he counted what money remained in his pocket. He had either owed money to those two men, or, more likely, Steve considered, the two men had been observing his success from the top of Town Street and had come to levy their own form of tax. The fairer man was simply a muscle man, there as a show of force. The sight was upsetting, yet fascinating. This was indeed "a dog eat dog world" – another expression frequently used by his science teacher.

Steve found Buzz outside the Corn Exchange. They queued for a burger and sat within the restaurant at a table of Formica and steel. Both boys stared idly out onto the street, satiating their hunger. The burger tasted good, though in some manner bland. Traffic thundered past beyond panes of glass that fell to the pavement. You could see the exhaust fumes thrumming on the tarmac.

"The recycling bloke says that places like this have developed their own type of potato," Steve absently said.

Buzz examined his chips with a frown. "What do you mean?"

"He says they've bred a potato that doesn't get any black bits, that is always more or less a certain size, and is ... you know, easier to make into chips ..."

"They've got to find something for their workers to do."

" ... and that sooner or later there'll just be one type of potato," Steve finished, "and we'll all have to eat it whether we like it or not."

"Then eat rice!"

"They shouldn't really dictate what we eat, should they?" Steve objected.

"Everywhere you look you get told what to do," Buzz argued, pointing at a bus that was passing, its side advertising a clothing outlet.

"But you've got a choice whether you buy their gear."

"Don't eat the chips then. You know you're putting me off my lunch, you."

"He does speak *some* sense," Steve admitted as they rose to leave.

"Who?"

"Robin: the recycling guy."

"Do you want to give this recycling bloke a rest?"

They made their way into Queen's Court, then straight up the escalator to Hedleys. Surprisingly, it was not busy for a Saturday. A strain of house music, not unlike the type Vinnie would approve of, kept your feet light, kept you shuffling up and down the aisles.

Mary-Anne had once explained her theory of clothing to Steve: the type of clothing you wore said a lot about your character; it was really no more than a means of self-expression, she had told him. Young people wore brighter colours: this was because they were more experimental, energetic and outgoing. Middle-aged people, their energies beginning to wane, tended to wear green and brown. Older folk wore grey, or more natural, earthy hues. The concept was almost depressing in its simplicity.

Steve studied the trainers on display, many of them costing in excess of a hundred pounds. The range astounded him. There was more variety here than there were strains of potato in the world! He handled one pair of grey suede edged with pink, fluorescent piping – a design that Anita might have favoured. Without really thinking, he raised it to his nose and breathed the smell of glue, rubber and fabric. It was that unmistakable "new" odour, a smell that told of money and of a new lease of life. Sometimes when Vinnie bought a shirt it came carefully packed with tissue paper folded into the creases. The crackle of discarded tissue had the same effect, the same association of luxury and expense.

There were still the same old gimmicks on sale, like shoes with lights embedded in their heels which flashed on and off as you walked. It brought a smile to Steve's lips: he had persuaded his mother to buy him a pair like that, and had been devastated when they had failed to work almost as soon as they got them home. "You've worn them now, they'll never exchange them," she had said, adamantly refusing to make a fuss.

Buzz emerged from the changing rooms. He had donned a shirt of electric blue. "What do you think then?"

"You look like something out of *Star Wars*!"

"Thanks, Steve. Thanks for the vote of confidence."

"You're welcome."

The two boys spent a further forty-five minutes in Hedleys. Buzz bought two shirts, paying ninety pounds with his debit card.

☙

"But I'm going to be holding the purse strings," Mary-Anne was saying in an attempt to dampen the atmosphere of wild excitement that pervaded the air.

"Course you are, my love. It's your house ..."

"I'll keep the bank book," Mary-Anne went on, eyes focusing on this scenario. "Yes, I'll be banker."

"And a very fine banker you'll make, too," Martin almost sang.

"We're rich, we're rich," Mary-Anne now shouted, giving herself over to the full force of her feelings. She took Steve by one hand and Martin by the other, and for a moment they danced about the room as they might around a Maypole. Then Mary-Anne threw herself onto the sofa, panting, red-faced. "Two hundred and forty-nine thousand," she murmured. "Who would ever have dreamt it?"

"Two hundred and forty-nine thousand and rising," Martin put in.

"Was that the valuation?" Steve questioned.

"On at two hundred and forty-nine thousand for offers in the region of two hundred and thirty-five," Martin explained. "Quite a big discount, that," he added with a half frown.

"We're rich," Mary-Anne kept muttering.

" ... and the beauty of it is we don't actually borrow a lump sum: we *draw down* the money when we need it."

"It's a very good way of doing it, isn't it?" Mary-Anne asked rhetorically.

"I can't think of a better way of doing it," Martin answered. "If you can, let me know."

As the level of excitement began to abate, so Steve was furnished with more details of their dealings with the bank. The surveyor had visited, at eleven, as arranged, but had only stayed for twenty minutes. "We would have no trouble with a house like this. It's just the kind of property we like to have on our books," he had said, apparently. Afterwards Mary-Anne and Martin had gone straight to the nearest branch in Seymour Street, where they had talked with a financial advisor for well over an hour and a half. There were forms to be filled out, a mandate to be signed. The account would be up and running within the month, with a facility to draw down eighty thousand pounds against Stanningley Terrace. The money could be accessed at any time – even over the Internet – and the loan redeemed at any point. In return for this the bank would charge two percentage points of interest over the Bank of England base rate. And for the duration of this arrangement the deeds to the house would be kept in the bank's vault at Head Office. What more could they ask for?

"What are the deeds?" Steve asked.

"The deeds prove ownership of property," Martin explained. "Without the deeds you can't really sell a house ... In fact, you *can't* sell it."

"So why does the bank keep them?"

"Simply to safeguard their interests. In the event of something going wrong they have the means to recoup the money they've loaned."

Steve frowned.

"But it's not going to come to that ... How could it?"

FOUR

Robin had got him himself into a bit of a muddle at the close of that morning's *toolbox talk*.

"We're not Evangelists, we shouldn't go around recruiting and preaching as such, but let's face it: we all get a bit of a lift working here, don't we? Otherwise we wouldn't be doing what we do. And you know what they say? *You only keep it by giving it away.*"

Nodding heads.

"So now that your fortnight has drawn to a close, Steve and Helena, I hope you will be able to go back to school and say that at least there was a generosity of spirit at *Pennine Recycling*. And that spirit, a vehicle of sorts, has enabled you to absorb some knowledge and information relating to the recycling industry, an industry which shall shortly be at the forefront of everyone's agenda."

Today Robin's ponytail was bound with an orange band. Steve thought this colour suited him better than the blue he had been wearing formerly.

"Is there anything you would like to say, Steve and Helena?" he asked.

Both teenagers shook their heads.

"Anything you feel we've left out? Any questions, in other words – or information? Yes, Steve ..."

Steve's expression was absolutely straight. "I don't feel I know enough about ozone depleting substances."

"CFCs, you mean? I'm not sure I know enough about them either," Robin replied with a laugh of false modesty. "But I'll dig out some literature for you later on."

Robin was true to his word. At four thirty that afternoon he handed Steve an article of three pages of stapled foolscap entitled "When a Hole is a Hole"; he also gave them each a white envelope on which he had written *Wentworth High School* in neat longhand. "Simply feedback," he explained.

Then it was time to part company. Helena shook hands with many of their fellow workers; Steve followed in her wake.

Robin was standing by the door. He gave them both a brief and light hug, more a show of solidarity than affection. There was a faint smell of oranges about Robin's lumberjack shirt.

"Good," he finished. "It's been a pleasure having you both here, that's all I can say. Thank you for your endeavours. Come and see us again soon."

Steve and Helena began to make their way back into town. The day had been hot – they had worked as if under a blanket of heat – and it did not seem any cooler outside the building. There were few pedestrians (for some reason the day at *Pennine Recycling* finished forty-five minutes earlier than the other units in the trading estate), but whatever pedestrians there were seemed possessed by a common languor.

"Well, that's that then," Steve murmured.

"Wasn't that bad, was it? Pretty good in fact." Helena returned.

"But what's this?" Steve then said, studying the white envelope afresh.

Helena did not answer.

"You going to open yours?" Steve asked her.

Helena shook her head.

"Well, I'm going to open mine."

And Steve eased open the gummed flap (organic glue, no doubt), shook open the letter, and read:

To whom it may concern

Steve has worked hard over his fortnight of work experience at *The Pennine Recycling Plant*. He has a practical nature, which he has used to good effect in handling the equipment here. He has interfaced well with the other workers. I would say, however, that an air of cynicism does underpin his outlook, which, one feels, prevents him from giving of himself fully. Compared with his fellow student there is evident a certain immaturity, perhaps consistent with his years. One wonders: what does Steve want out of life? Forgive me writing to you in this manner, but we have found that an experiment without feedback can prove to be of limited value.

Yours ever,
Robin Fellowes

"Cheeky, pompous bugger," Steve whispered.

"What does it say?"

"' ... *an air of cynicism underpins his outlook, which, one feels, prevents him from giving of himself fully*'. He wants a slap!"

"Here: let me have a look ..."

"No way."

They struggled together briefly, but Steve managed to keep Robin's report well out of reach. As Helena pulled on tiptoes at his outstretched arm he smelt the warmth of her breath on his neck.

"Going to read yours, then?"

"Not addressed to me, is it?"

"Bet you've got a rave ... teacher's pet!"

Presently they turned right to cut through the Kellforth Estate. This would bring them to a main road from which Helena could catch a bus home. They were walking downhill now and almost at once a view of the valley bottom opened up ahead of them.

A game of cricket was in progress at the Kellforth Cricket Club. Edmund Marsden had played for the local team for two seasons, and Steve looked on with idle interest. The players were walking in well with the bowler, the miniature figures in white resembling the fronds of an invertebrate, moving independently yet with a common purpose and direction. The bowler, however, could improve his run-up and action: he seemed to steam in from well over twenty paces out only to decelerate in a muddle of misplaced steps just outside the crease. And the first slip was too far forward of the keeper: no doubt he was trying to emulate the example of a first-class cricketer voted *Man of the Match* in the Test Match at Trent Bridge last week.

"Is that the kind of place you're going to end up in?" Steve asked of his companion, gesturing behind them.

"At *Pennine Recycling*? No, I'm going to university, or I want to go to university."

"To do what?"

"Marine biology."

"To save the oceans?"

There was a note of seriousness in Helena's reply. "Certainly going to try."

"You're not going to make your fortune doing that."

"Don't want to make a fortune. I'm happy with just enough."

"So am I," Steve quickly added.

"The planet's in a sorry state, and it's chasing money that does it," Helena went on, almost as if she were talking to herself.

"You sound like Robin!"

Then she stopped and said: "Your father's dead, isn't he?"

"Yes – he died when I was three."

"'Cos my dad's got cancer, see. That's why I'm into all this. He was at Hessops as a chemical engineer for twenty years. That's three of them now on the plant that's got leukaemia." Her eyes were brighter, yet her voice remained unaltered. "And Hessops just don't care. You should see the letters we get from their lawyer people. It's only money they're interested in: they don't care who they tread on."

They walked the next one hundred metres in silence. Steve did not know what to say. What *could* he say? He certainly could not ask her out on a date now, which had earlier been his intention. But when he did speak, his words were, if anything, more spontaneous than they might otherwise have been.

"I'd like to see you again, you know ..."

She glanced up at him, held his eyes, then grinned: "You're not my type, remember: too cynical."

"I'm not *really*."

"You are!"

"Let me show you."

Helena was at once serious again. "At the moment ... well, it's not the right time, with my dad and all."

"I understand."

"A time will come though," she said, "but only if you promise not *to give of yourself fully* ..."

ॐ

Mrs Holland had a bowl of lilies beside the window today – not StarGazers, like Mary-Anne sometimes bought, but white lilies, the stamens a yolk yellow before the waxy petals.

"And you've been in Amsterdam?" Mrs Holland asked of Vinnie.

"That's right."

"Behaved yourself, I hope."

"Like I always do."

There was a brief silence. The old lady seemed to be weighing something up in her mind, glancing from one brother to the other. Then she drew a deep breath; as she did so her eyes appeared to soften in intensity.

"I've asked you both to come and see me today because ... well, I wanted to give you this ..."

She withdrew two pieces of folded paper from under the pillow to her left. She proffered these to her guests, one each. The two boys stepped forwards. Steve saw at once that Mrs Holland had handed him a cheque. He glanced uncertainly at Vinnie, who had unfolded his, and who appeared to be repeatedly rereading the instructions. Steve looked down to his hand. The cheque was for the sum of £1,250.

Vinnie spoke for them both. "What's this?" he asked.

"It's a gift," Mrs Holland simply replied. "It's a gift from me to you."

"For what, though?" Vinnie persevered.

"For being you, both of you. I've known you since you were born. I was after all a friend of your grandparents. As you know I was very fond of Edmund, very fond. And I feel I am in my right to do whatever I want with my money." She raised both hands clear of the bedclothes. "So I'm giving some of it to you."

"Thank you, Mrs Holland," Steve stammered. "I had no idea ..."

"Yes, thank you," Vinnie mumbled.

"When you get to my age everyone seems to be in a hurry to part you from your possessions. They take your house, your furniture, even your books. This is all there is now. " She waved vaguely over the room before her. "So it's nice to be able to beat them to it on occasions, if for no other reason than to have the upper hand."

She paused before continuing.

"Of course I've spoken to Mary-Anne ... I wouldn't have dreamt of doing anything like this without her knowledge. But you are to understand one thing: that there are absolutely no strings attached," Mrs Holland went on, more serious now. "You can do whatever you want with the money without thinking you'll upset me." She paused again before continuing. "I would remind you of one thing, however ..."

"Yes ..." one of the brothers whispered.

"I don't want to sound melodramatic – but don't bury your talents in the sand."

Both nodded.

"You know the parable?"

"Yes, Mrs Holland."

"Because there's nothing worse than burying things in the sand ... The only things that should be buried in the sand are the likes of my mortal remains when I'm gone."

Steve always tried to remonstrate when Mrs Holland spoke in this manner. She waved him down.

"Anyway I've said my piece. I just want you both to *live* your lives, realising all that potential in you. Because you've both got a great deal of potential. This is a gesture to encourage that. I'm stuck here: I can't do anything. This is all I can do. I know it's only small – but it's a way – my way – of saying *get out there and do it*."

❧

Steve and Martin had taken the car over to a mechanic friend to have some new brake pads fitted and now, on their way home, they were on a fact-finding expedition in the Bolton Hill area. Martin drove slowly, with his arm crooked over the steering wheel; that way he could lean right forwards, apparently gaining a better position from which to survey the streets of identical houses.

"These houses were all built in the Thirties," he was saying. "Look at the garages: designed for vehicles of a different era. You could drive into them in this car, but you wouldn't open the doors."

The image of them imprisoned within the car brought a smile to Steve's lips. "So they're not really garages, then?"

"Glorified tool sheds."

What was remarkable was the absence of trees. And then when there was a tree it would be something unsuitable, like a monkey-puzzle, black, sharp and coniferous, or a willow, famous for causing subsidence with its "extended zone of influence", as Martin termed it. The streets seemed to go on forever without providing a surprise. All the houses had bay windows, downstairs and up; all had drives leading to identical garages (in fact there were some dissimilarities here as some owners had block-paved their drives, others tarmacced the once concreted surface); each dwelling was a mirror image of its twin. The only original variation of design seemed to be in the front doors – some had portholes for windows, others rectangles of glass on end in the Art Deco style – and the leaded lights (although the vast majority of these were replicas in PVC frames). A young lady was crossing the road ahead. As they approached, she kept looking over her shoulder, as if haunted by the hesitancy of their passage.

"Alright, darling; don't panic," Martin muttered. "I'm not looking at your bust, I'm looking at your house."

But there was something depressed in Martin's manner. After their euphoria on getting the bank's commitment to lend money against Stanningley Terrace, there had followed a lull. This was due in part to what Mary-Anne called "the 'what goes up must come down' factor"; it was also born of worry and anxiety – as if, now he had secured what was needed to fuel his ambitions, so now the time was upon him to deliver. Perhaps the endless unfolding of these streets of semi-detached houses did not help.

"You going to get one of these, then?" Steve asked eventually.

"No, no, no. Just market research, this. We're here to see the whole picture."

"What do you mean?"

"We need to see what's going on across the board. No, we're going to buy something in town. A flat for young professionals. We don't want to be dealing with families."

"What's wrong with families?"

"No money. No style."

Ahead there was a skip parked up on the pavement with a sheet of tarpaulin stretched tight over its corners. They pulled up alongside it. Building materials – a heap of sand, concrete flags stacked on end, some timber – had been positioned neatly within the confines of a front garden. The contractor had affixed his sign directly over the front door: *Room with a View, Loft Conversions of Excellence.*

Martin grimaced. "Quite a tidy site," was all he offered.

FIVE

There were no flies on Vinnie. The next day he had banked his cheque, and in the time it had taken for the funds to clear, he had carried out all the market research that was required. Orders for stock had then been placed on the Internet, and not long after packages had begun to arrive in earnest – some registered delivery, others bound with tape, addressed in biro and sporting foreign stamps.

And now, three weeks on, he was in business. It all seemed so effortless. The only thing strange was the fact that no one in the market seemed to pay the blindest bit of attention. The ubiquitous green leaf of the cannabis plant, this one printed onto a bath towel and hung like a flag from the steel frame at the back of Vinnie's stall, could have been there since time immemorial.

The display of Vinnie's wares reminded Steve of a firework shop a neighbour had taken him to when he was five or six. Then he had stared through the glass cabinet at the Rockets, Roman Candles and Catherine Wheels, intoxicated by the oriental motifs and smell of gunpowder. Now he turned the pipes of carved teak over and over between inquisitive fingers, caressed the soapstone chillums, definitely soapy to the touch, and caught sight of his distorted reflection in the glass bongs as he rotated these, too, fathoming the transparent passage of smoke from bowl to lungs.

"This one's my favourite; it's Californian," Vinnie said, dismantling a pipe of brass into four separate pieces: a rod for poking; a capped tube for stashing; a removable bottom to give access for cleaning, and the pipe itself. It was indeed a well-engineered piece, the components fitting snugly together, each locking its predecessor into position.

"How much is it?" Steve asked.

"You don't smoke, remember?"

"Christ, Vinnie! Twenty-five quid? You'll never get that."

"Sold two yesterday."

It did appear that, compared to the other stalls in this open-air part of the town's market, Vinnie's stock was dear. Next door, for instance, was a stall displaying stationery, toys and cassettes. Whilst Vinnie was talking to a client, Steve had rummaged through the cassettes: *Charlie Pride's Greatest Hits* for £1.50, *All I have to Do is Dream* by the Everley Brothers for £2. This man would have to sell a dozen tapes to realise the value of one pipe. Two stalls to the left a woman was selling second-hand clothes, in reality a tangle of used clothing heaped onto a barrow. "That's 50p, love." Directly opposite a stall advertised pet food and pet accessories: *Pigs Ear 50p*; *Dog Basket £3.50*. Again, that stallholder would have to work all day to take what Vinnie was turning over before lunch.

And from what Vinnie had led him to believe, the mark-up on his type of goods was handsome: buying ten brass pipes wholesale had brought the price down to twelve pounds each. But what was perhaps most gratifying of all was the fact that Vinnie was taking it completely in his stride: he looked about him with a grave, serious expression, which spoke not of worry, but of the fact that here was a man with business on his mind. All along he had been a man of commerce. His dealings with the council employee collecting rent for the stall exemplified this.

"Going alright, is it?"

"Can't complain."

"There's a bloke selling all this stuff in Harrogate Market. Got more kit than you, though ..."

"I'll get there, don't worry. What's the tax?"

"That's fourteen quid."

"Don't I get a special introductory rate?"
"Do you heck."

And all the while there was a background of music, not Vinnie's usual blend of Acid House, but a reggae beat, tailored to cater for his punters:

> *Then we would cook corn meal porridge*
> *Of which I'll share with you*
> *My feet is my only carriage*
> *So I've got to push on thro.*

What became apparent some time later – a fact that Vinnie had not seen fit formerly to disclose – was that there was a partner in this venture: Rich Swift. Vinnie may have kept quiet about Rich's involvement on account of his wanting to take all the glory, in his own and Steve's eyes, for the instant success of this brisk trade; it may also have been an effort on his part to keep his friend out of the picture for as long as possible. Rich was not all bad, but he had a reputation – there had been run-ins with the police, one resulting in an accident with a moped (he walked now with a limp) – and it would take some time for memories to fail, or for the next generation of his like to assume the position he had so quickly and willingly attained. Rich had a winning smile, but he had typically offset this by having a gold eyetooth fitted: he looked like a pirate.

"Yes, Steve," he grinned. "You okay? You like our shop?"

And he spilt the contents of a plastic carrier bag – wallets, money belts, hair bands and eye patches (the type used by passengers on long haul flights) – over the table at the back of the stall. All had labels that read: *100% hemp cloth exterior. Made in Thailand.* And all had stitched somewhere on the bleached material the dark green leaf, seven fronded, like a starburst in emerald.

"Excellent, Rich," Vinnie breathed. "These'll walk out of here."

"The wallets three pounds fifty, the bands two pounds."

"No, no: four pounds fifty and three pounds."

As Steve made his way into town later on that morning, he thought of Mrs Holland's talents in the sand and he smiled. The fact was, she would most probably be proud of Vinnie. He was breaking no laws: in fact, by taking rent, the council was pretty much underwriting the enterprise, legally and morally. He was not sure if Mary-Anne was aware that Rich was involved: that would come later. But if the business were up and running by then, Vinnie would not need her approval. He could hear him intoning "Muuum ... Leave it!" Vinnie had always seen fit to act independently of his mother, much more so than Steve ever had dared. Perhaps he, Steve, should be more his own man, he absently reflected.

He was by now at the bottom end of town, near the bus station. At the next cash dispenser he checked his balance: £1,410.56. This represented Mrs Holland's gift, the balance being birthday money and pocket money accrued. He withdrew sixty pounds without a receipt, thinking he might treat himself to a shirt he had seen in Benetton with Buzz some days before. As he made his way along the canal, the banks of cumulus clouds mirrored faithfully on the glass-like water, he considered his capital.

It was not easy to know how best to utilise it. "You might get four-and-a-half percent in a deposit account," Martin had grunted when the two brothers had returned from Greenglades with their cheques; "... if you're lucky. Let's see," he had gone on with a calculator, "4.5% on £1,250: that's £56.25 a year – the princely sum of £1.08 per week ... and that's gross. But you're not a tax payer, are you?" he finished with a laugh. Depressed by this fact Steve had left the money languishing in his current account, where it attracted no interest at all. There were stocks and shares. But which ones? He had read an article on the Internet for young investors who were considering the stock market: the advice was to "buy shares in companies you like": McDonalds, Nike, Adidas etc. Not exactly inspiring stuff.

~

"This property will be gone by the weekend," the agent was saying. "We had more than six offers on it when it first came on in May. Now that it's back on the market, and at the same price, I can't see it remaining unsold beyond Friday."

Martin was listening intently, nodding his head, lips puckered. He was making a show of scrutinising the agent, as if to say "I've got the measure of you." Yet you could see the mounting tension on his face, written over knitted brows. The agent knew how to deal with this type of client, however: he kept moving between rooms.

"And why has it come back on the market, in fact?" Martin asked, trying to engage the other's eyes.

"Chain broke two links back," came the simple reply, ringing over bare floorboards, echoing through an empty hall. "As you can see, the vendor has moved out ... to a property in Cumbria, I'm told. He's in no hurry to sell, but he's instructed us to take the first decent offer that comes along."

"We *are* cash buyers ... or, rather, I am a cash buyer," Martin corrected himself with a grin in Steve's direction.

"So I understand, Mr Lenton."

"And it's on at sixty-eight?"

"Sixty-eight thousand seven hundred and fifty pounds."

"I'm not sure it's quite what we're looking for," Martin then said, and he walked purposefully through the hall to the kitchen at the rear of the flat. Steve followed, only he entered the back bedroom.

This was the top floor of a terraced house, close to the centre of town. The view was spectacular. There seemed to be a natural basin below, in the centre of which stood a gasometer. Around this giant structure, like arteries from a pumping heart, a series of main roads radiated, carrying a substantial volume of cars and wagons, from here so minuscule you could have been passing overhead in an aeroplane. From the pit of this basin the streets, a patchwork of red-tiled roofs punctuated by a number of taller, more modern buildings, rose on all sides to the horizon. Directly below the window there was a communal garden of sorts. This had been allowed to fall into a state of disarray: indeed the far end was no more than a rubbish tip. Magpies had colonised the silver birches that formed the perimeter of this area. Steve could hear their evil cawing but not see them: the trees were so full of leaf he could only trace their passage in the shaking branches as they crashed about like baboons.

"What *are* you looking for?" he heard the agent ask of Martin.

"I'll know it when I see it," was the answer.

Steve wandered aimlessly from room to room. The vendor had done a good job of clearing the flat; in one room there was a copy of the *Yellow Pages*, in another a small coffee table; otherwise the rooms were bare. There was a dry, dusty smell – no window had been opened for months. Surely there was not enough work to do in this flat? It was more of a buy-to-rent proposition. As they drove to the next property, Martin concurred with this line of thought.

"We're looking for a dog's dinner," he said.

"Really?"

"Yes, a right old mess."

And a dog's dinner, a "garden" flat – set some feet below ground level, but not a basement – was exactly what they next found. The agent had entrusted them with the key to this property. Perhaps it had been on the market for so long it was thought not to warrant valuable selling time. They must return the key sometime tomorrow.

"This is more like it," Martin murmured, as he pushed open the front door against a weight of letters and mail shots. "We'll have to watch our step here, there's no light."

There were shutters to the street side and once folded back on their hinges a half-light, almost a twilight, seemed to glow within the walls. Unlike the last, this flat was still furnished, though all personal effects had been removed: empty drawers were stuck crookedly open, shelves were bare. Steve paced about with a growing interest, for here was the shell, the husk of someone's life. He stood before a calendar, which hung from a nail over the fireplace. It was November's page, with an image of leafless trees standing black on a riverbank, a spaceless sky beyond. Someone had been crossing off the days, but the crosses finished at the 23rd.

"Do you think this person died?" Steve asked of Martin, and his words seemed to be lost in the mildew of the soft furnishings.

"A goner, yep. Nothing wrong with that: sometimes a bonus when they die *in situ* – puts people off."

"Been on the market a while ..."

Martin was staring at the wall that divided front and back rooms. "Just waiting for someone with a bit of vision," he intoned, knocking from top to bottom with his knuckles.

Steve paused by the entrance to the toilet. The bowl, as much as he could see of it, was stained brown, caked with excrement; the linoleum tiles below were bleached, cracked and curling away from the concrete underneath. The bathroom was no better. The suite was yellow with water stains beneath each of the four taps. The open door of an airing cupboard to the right of the bath revealed egg-blue wallpaper within, decorated in a *Festival of Britain* style with miniature sceptres and coronets. The paste had long given out and the paper hung like jungle foliage. The whole effect was, to Steve's mind, creepy, unnerving.

"Where there's muck there's money, eh Steve?" Martin laughed, reading his stepson's expression.

"I don't like it, Martin: it's as if it's ... haunted."

"Once it's cleared out you'll see the difference," and Martin clicked his fingers.

As they drove home Steve pondered that last statement. It was almost as if Martin had set his heart on that property and need see no others. In fact he more or less said as much.

"I think we're in business," he murmured. "Location: tick. Size of rooms: tick. Potential: most definitely. Price: TBA ..."

Then, pulling up the car, he finished: "Got to get some pasta for your mother – carbonara night tonight – and just nip in there ..."

"What? There, you mean?" Steve questioned, gesturing in the direction of the bookie's.

"Winnings, Steven, old man – winnings."

"Go on."

"Yes, and at Windsor of all places ..."

As Martin disappeared into the grocer's Steve scrutinised the front of the bookmaker's. There were six panels illustrating different sports: a diving goalie; two horses, one winning by a nose; a tennis player reaching for the ball; greyhounds in full flight; two swimmers simultaneously taking a breath between strokes of front crawl; a batsman performing a square cut, as if to extra cover. The images were coloured in block-like form, like a silk screen. In one part of the window a series of posters advertised odds. Steve's gaze alighted on the one headed *Fifth Test*: *England v West Indies at The Oval*. There were two columns, one entitled *10 Wicket Innings*, the other *Centuries*. Steve's eyes traced the surnames of the bowlers: Fairclough, Davenport, Pollock; then those of the batsmen: Richert, Levine, Orme. Beside each name the odds had been listed; for example, beside Davenport and Pollock were scrawled 20-1 and 16-1; and alongside Levine and Orme, 12-1 and 33-1 respectively. Steve looked long and hard. Davenport was not such a bad bet: his meteoric progress up through the ranks to first class cricket had been eagerly anticipated by the nation, several million people willing this young man, barely out of his teens, on to success. Nor was Levine a bad bet either: on a good day it was hard to see this batsman being dismissed, and if he was timing his strokes well, there would be a bucket-full of boundaries.

Steve felt his heart kick and the blood smart in his veins. He got out of the car and crossed the road to stand in front of the poster. There was no other name which demanded special attention; but the more he gazed at the lettering in magic marker the more sure he was of Davenport and Levine. He moved now to stand beside the open door of the bookmakers. It was dim inside; there were perhaps four people standing next to a counter which faced the street, beneath lettering on a glass panel which read: *Pay Out*. All the while, there was the commentary of a horse race in progress: *"And as they come now to the final furlong it's Mystic Major who takes it up from Hanna's Girl and Intrepido, Solar Century under pressure ... It's Mystic Major who goes on with Give Me Strength making good headway ... It's Mystic Major from Give Me Strength kicking on ... It's Mystic ..."*

Here the commentator's voice reached a new pitch; this seemed to disperse those punters at the counter, who now paced about, their eyes either fixed to a screen out of view, or glued to the floor.

"Up towards the line and it's Mystic Major from Give Me Strength, Hanna's Girl dropping out of contention ...it's Mystic Major and Give Me Strength: they're running in a line ... it's Mystic Major from Give Me Strength, there's nothing between them ..."

And now shouting from within. "Go on, Mystic Major ... go on ..."

"They've gone past together: photo Sandown ..."

More shouting from within. "Bollocks ..."

When the commentator's voice resumed over the tannoy its tone had returned to normal: no longer was there a ring of frenzy or of anticipation. For some reason the contrast between the two brought a smile to Steve's lips: these voices could have been belonged to two different people. *"Photo, Sandown, between number three, Mystic Major and number eight, Give Me Strength ... They're going down Lingfield: they bet ..."*

"Oi, oi." It was Martin.

"Martin, I want to have a bet."

"You'll have me shot."

Steve withdrew two ten pound notes from his back pocket, and

gestured at the cricket prices. "Davenport and Levine."
"You *sure*?"
"I'm sure."

SIX

Buzz, Mel, Anita and Steve had been in Rangefields Park. They had drunk a Bacardi Breezer each and two bottles of Grolsch between them. Then Steve had gone to the shop to get a packet of gum – the alcohol tasted dry on his tongue – and when he came back ... Buzz and Mel were an item.

It had been embarrassing to watch them lying side by side, Buzz's hand caressing the small of Mel's back; and when they rolled over, with Buzz on top, Steve found he had to look away as their mouths met. There was also the added tension of Anita and Steve *not* being an item: one moment the four of them had been equals, the next there were two odd ones out – gooseberries both.

And now as they skirted town – the idea was to go bowling – that tension was just as pronounced. Buzz and Mel walked in front, sometimes hand in hand, at other times with an arm wrapped around each other's waist, or more precisely, in Buzz's case, a hand digging into the back pocket of Mel's jeans. Anita was not in the least embarrassed: a smile played on her lips and one eyebrow was held high as she matched Steve's step stride for stride.

Soon they were passing the hospital. There was more activity here and they had to negotiate the closely parked cars and anticipate the direction of people as they made their way purposefully to the infirmary's various departments. Buzz and Mel had stopped beneath the type of sign you might associate with a holiday camp, its white arrows describing the myriad schools of medicine: *Endocrinology; Haematology; Prosthetics; Neurology; Orthopaedic Outpatients*. Buzz was pointing at a sign that read *Sexual Health*.

"Perfectly healthy me, thank you very much," he said.

Mel held her chin close to her neck as if to say "Should hope so too".

They walked on. Perhaps he, Steve, should take Anita's hand. It was expected of him, certainly, but beyond that it might be fun. He could imagine her thumb stroking his knuckles, sense her shoulder rubbing against his own. He could "hear" the clunk of their hips touching momentarily as they stepped from a curb. Then, when they got to the bowling alley, they might even kiss.

Just as he was considering this last scenario, he felt Anita's fingers searching for his own, then the firmness of her grip over the breadth of his hand. At first he acted dumb, as if he could not work out what had happened, and averted his eyes towards the sky, where dozens of swallows and house martins wheeled madly like insects. Then he looked awkwardly down at the pavement beneath his feet, and then finally at Anita. Her eyes burnt with a purpose and intensity he had not witnessed before. It was almost alarming. He glanced away towards the white steps of the Brodley Wing entrance of the hospital.

And saw Helena.

Their eyes met at the same instant. Both smiled openly at one another, but whereas Steve's smile was prolonged and constant, Helena's expression of bright surprise died a slow and withering death. She appeared by turns confused, hurt and then irritated. Instinctively Steve tried to remove his hand from Anita's grasp; but found he was held tight. Nevertheless, he stopped in his tracks. Anita made a show of being a puppet, returning to Steve's side as if on elastic.

"Helena, hi," Steve stammered.

"Hi ..."

"What are you doing?" he stupidly asked.

"Seeing my dad."

There was no more to be said; indeed there was no more that

could be said under the circumstances. And especially as Buzz and Mel were making their way back up the street. Steve had by now extricated his hand from Anita's and was silently gesturing. But no words were forthcoming. Helena gave one last, awkward smile, shrugged as if to indicate that she, too, did not know what to say either, and was on her way. It had all happened so quickly.

By the time they had reached the bottom of the street, Anita had taken Steve's hand once again. "Poor Helena," she said. "Her father's not well is he?"

"No, he's not."

"What's up with him?"

"He's got something from work ..."

Well, that was bloody that, Steve thought with emphasis as they walked on, yet he was not prepared to relinquish a picture indelibly scored on his mind's eye of Helena's expression of confusion and hurt. His beautiful Helena! How could he have subjected her to that? How he wished he could turn back the clock. Or how he wished he could be with her now, explaining himself, excusing himself. But there was no future in these last speculations: that door was stuck fast, as if slammed by an autumn wind: there would be no opening it now. His overriding desire was to kick the curb to vent his frustration and disappointment. But this option was not open to him either. How had it all happened? It just didn't seem possible.

Buzz and Mel had walked into a shop selling diving accessories and wetsuits, newly opened. Anita broke hands and joined them. Steve stood before the shop front, absently staring at his reflection, which trembled each time the heavier vehicles thundered passed on the tarmac behind. On the other side of the glass a life-size dummy in full diving regalia was held horizontal by wires attached to the ceiling, arms rigid at its waist. Directly below this rubber-suited man was a shelf on which a bag of pebbles had been spilt and raked. Someone had positioned a number of starfish over these stones to complete the effect. The shop was quite a magnet: many people were pacing about within, against a backdrop of sea-green walls.

Steve's eyes focused on Anita as she stood before a stand of postcards. Had she seen Helena emerge from the hospital and *then* taken his hand, he was asking of himself; thus effectively capitalising on the chance meeting, and engineering this impasse? Or had events merely unfolded of their own accord, ordained by fate? He could not be sure. The only thing he knew for certain was that Helena was gone. It was as if he had been on a train and had failed to get off at his stop; now the train was thundering ahead, the places, the people he was meant to be amongst, receding into the distance.

It was almost as if Anita could read Steve's mind, since all the way to the bowling alley she kept her distance from him. Not once did her hand or shoulder touch his; not once did she stumble on her heels and reach out for support. Paradoxically this made Steve feel even more anxious: not only had he lost Helena, now Anita was gone – in a minute he would have no one. He was shocked by the fragility and vulnerability of his position. And shocked by his own weakness, as he understood it, in viewing it in this way. Again the image of the train suggested itself to him. He had "left something behind" certainly, and he could not now return to retrieve it; instead he must make out in this new landscape. Whilst Buzz and Mel left them for a few moments to withdraw cash from an ATM, Steve pulled Anita to him with both hands.

"Steve ..."

ॐ

"I'm going to spec up this flat something rotten," Martin was boasting later that night as they sat before the television. "The guy who buys it isn't going to want to come out of it."

"Or the girl," Mary-Anne countered.

"It's a boy's flat, isn't it, Steve?"

Steve shrugged.

"What's a boy's flat, then?" Mary-Anne asked.

"Well, it's not the type of flat you'd have a baby in ..."

"What a lot of rubbish you talk, Martin! How do you know what kind of a flat a girl wants to have a baby in?"

Martin raised both hands as if in surrender. "Okay, okay. Do you know what? I'll keep an open mind: I don't mind who buys it so long as we make a few quid ... or more than a few quid," he finished, quieter.

"And am I going to see the flat?" Mary-Anne asked. "After all, I'm in charge of the ..."

"I'm just doing an artist's impression of it now ..."

"I'll need to see more than that."

Martin had been hard at it, as he called it, all evening. It was agreed that no formal business plan as such was needed since no one other than Mary-Anne was required to sanction the release of funds. But she would want to see a comprehensive break down of costs and a forecast of the profit margin. If she was satisfied, then that was all that mattered. Mary-Anne's wish was that Steve was to have some involvement: it would be a good learning experience and introduction to business. Martin clearly welcomed this, since he saw Steve as a conduit of influence to Mary-Anne. And Steve welcomed it, too; it made him feel his opinions were valued.

"Right, I think I'm ready," Martin announced with a note of feigned exhaustion. "Ready for the bank's scrutiny!"

"We just want to get it right," Mary-Anne said as the three of them took their places around the table from which they normally ate.

"So here we are," Martin went on, straightening as if he were at a business conference. "I have listed here the improvements I intend to make to the property ... against which you will see two columns: one a bill of materials, the other a labour figure. This labour figure refers to outside contractors," he grandly pronounced. "Of course, as everyone is well aware, I am the chief labour element, but my remuneration will be an element contained within the overall profit of the enterprise ..."

"Oh, Martin, what do you mean? Why are you using all these expressions?"

" ... which put more simply means that cost of goods sold – i.e. materials plus labour – will not include my time: I shall not be paying myself a salary ..."

"You mean *I* won't be paying you a salary?"

"Mary-Anne, will you let me finish? All I'm trying to say is that the profit made at the end of the day will be inflated insofar as I will not have been paid. Put more simply: if we were paying someone else to do the work I shall be doing, the profit margin, when the property is disposed of, would be smaller."

"But you will be doing the work, won't you?"

"Of course I will," Martin replied, now with an air of irritation. "I think we should move on to more specific issues."

"What's going out and what's coming in?" Mary-Anne asked. "That's all that concerns me."

"Good, right: well, what's going out is the following," and he spun a pad of foolscap over the tabletop. There were three columns in point of fact: the left-hand column was headed *Improvements*, and the two to the right *Materials* and *Labour*. Two vertical lines of biro delineated them, bringing this spreadsheet of sorts into better definition. Martin had listed the following in his column of *Improvements*: bathroom; kitchen; flooring; electric; plumbing (heating); French windows; garden landscaping; decoration. Against each sub-heading, exactly as he had just explained, he had written a price for *Materials* and *Labour*. Thus against plumbing he had written £800 and £550; against flooring he had written £450 but no labour element – in this instance it seemed he intended to fit the floor without assistance. The total *Materials* bill was £8,250; the total *Labour* £1,800. Then he had added the two totals together and applied a factor of ten percent.

"What's that, then?" Mary-Anne asked over her spectacles.

"That's what's known as a cushion."

"So which figure are we looking at?"

There was a note of exasperation in Martin's answer. "Well, strictly speaking we should be looking at the total costs without the ten percent; but for the purposes of an estimate it is always worth having a cushion."

"Why should we need a cushion if we've got our figures right?"

"Because we might be half way through the job and think: wait a minute, let's up the spec of the bathroom suite; or perhaps we might want to fit the French windows with hardwood as opposed to softwood frames. Or ..."

"You mean it's for when you change your mind?"

"All these kind of jobs have a certain element of 'suck it and see', Mary-Anne."

Surprisingly to Steve, his mother seemed satisfied with this. "So what are the overall costs? Ten thousand and fifty pounds plus ten percent: Eleven thousand and fifty-five pounds? Is that right?"

"Correct."

"And we're buying the flat for what?"

"The sixty million dollar question."

Now she looked puzzled. "Martin, I want to make some notes of my own. Will you just tell me in plain English what you're intending to pay for the flat and then what you think you'll get for it when it's finished?"

"Well, I propose we make an offer of fifty-two thousand with a view to selling it three months later for seventy-two thousand. That's about right, isn't it, Steve?"

Steve shrugged. "Don't ask me," he replied.

"You've been around some of the flats with me; you've got an idea."

"I think it could be quite nice once it's done," Steve now pronounced, picturing the bathroom with its peeling wallpaper and the window shutters hanging open. "But what about your idea of joining the two rooms together?"

"That's over and above this," Martin answered, pointing at the pad. "If we go down that road, we'll exceed this projection."

"You've lost me," Mary-Anne sighed.

"Well, over and above all these improvements which *must* be made, there is an optional improvement which we *could* make: this." And he proudly turned a page on the pad. "Voila!"

And here was an isometric view of the front and back rooms knocked together, as seen from the street side, a view of the garden clearly visible through a low rectangular window on the back wall. Martin had even drawn a series of shrubs beyond a closely cropped lawn to complete the picture.

"Heavens!" Mary-Anne exclaimed.

"It seems to me, " Martin explained, "that we are in the enviable position of not having to commit ourselves to this modification until such a time as we're in there, tearing the place apart. But my forecasts, conservative forecasts, indicate that costings of approximately eighteen hundred pounds could put as much as five thousand on the selling price. It would just take the whole thing to a different level."

Mary-Anne was studying Martin, then the sketch. "How do you do it?" she asked eventually.

"Easy when you know how ... basically two pillars from original brick here," he explained with the point of his biro, "a beam spanning the two, make good the plasterwork and the job's a good 'un."

"It would have to be a strong beam," Mary-Anne absently remarked.

"Of course it would have to be strong – RSJ strong. Obviously we'd get a structural engineer in to do all the loadings and calcs."

"Oh well, in that case ..." Mary-Anne nodded, as if granting a concession of some kind.

Then a moment later, with more purpose in her voice, she made her judgement: "Right, I think that's a perfectly good business plan. So where are we? We have a facility to borrow eighty; we said we'd not go over seventy. You've got twelve thousand here including your beam affair. Let's offer fifty thousand."

"I said fifty-two thousand."

"And I say fifty thousand."

"My, you're a hard woman!"

They returned to their seats. Legs pushed well forwards, one on top of the other, Martin seemed very pleased with the way things had gone. Whereas before he would have laid himself out on the sofa and could well be asleep by now – snoring even – this evening he was possessed of a different energy. This energy had transmitted itself to Mary-Anne as well: if Martin was happy, then she was happy.

Steve, for his part, was tired. Through half-shut eyes he absently focused on the flickering screen of the television where a gasometer, similar to the one he had viewed from the top floor of that terraced house, seemed to be the object of attention. He considered the day's events; rather, he passed over the day by way of reliving the spectrum of feelings he had experienced: Anita's fingers exploring his own; Helena's smile closing like a flower; the kiss at the bowling alley, like a dam bursting; again Anita's fingers, this time gently massaging his hips. He closed his eyes: you could fast-forward these images or rewind them at will; it did not matter if they were out of sequence. You could even freeze them. All the while a television reporter was speaking, his words rising and falling like the sea. *"The West Indies were forced to follow on at lunch ... Another outstanding performance by the young man from Yorkshire: one hundred and thirty-four not out ..."*

Steve lifted one eyelid, like a reptile. The gasometer had moved to top left, revealing the immaculately prepared outfield of The

Oval.

"And a ten-wicket innings for the Surrey pace bowler Andrew Davenport: ten for ninety-eight, which brings him now centre stage in the arena of international cricket ..."

And here the scorecard of statistics was replaced by a series of falling wickets: LBW without playing a shot; off stump out of the ground twice; caught at extra cover; LBW trapped plumb on the back foot; a series of catches taken with clinical precision by second and third slips; a yorker which took the centre stump cartwheeling towards the keeper; and finally a wild hook by a tail-ender, the ball caught at deep square leg. Each time Davenport punched the air as if he were performing an uppercut.

Steve was by now on the edge on his chair. He needed to see the batting card again to confirm Levine's score – just to make sure. Martin looked up, as if to silently chastise his stepson for bringing him out of his warm reflections. Then there it was, clear as day: B. Levine: one hundred and thirty four not out.

"Yes," Steve hissed.

Martin frowned and silently questioned the other's exclamation with a turn of the wrist.

Steve began to delve into his back pocket. The betting office receipt was not there. Had he lost it at the bowling alley? Then it was there: between his shaking fingers. He waved it at Martin. Immediately recognising the pink slip and carbon lettering, he gestured like a policeman to the door.

"I did it," Steve breathed once they were alone.

"You bloody didn't?"

"I did. Look!"

"Christ ... you have and all."

"Levine and Davenport."

Martin's expression was dull and blank.

"What is it?" Steve begged. "What's wrong?"

"Wrong? There's nothing wrong. Twenty-to-one and twelve-to-one. You've won yourself three hundred and twenty pounds."

"You're joking me?"

"I'm not, old son. Three hundred and twenty pounds is what you've won."

Steve was speechless. There was a timeless pause.

"And if you'd done a double, a ten pound double," Martin went on, "with these prices you would have won ... over two thousand, five hundred pounds ..."

"What?"

"An accumulator: the winnings from one bet going onto the next. A tenner on twenty-to-one would put two hundred and ten pounds onto the twelve-to-one ... Serious money."

"Bloody hell," Steve stammered. "I didn't realise the bookies paid out that kind of cash."

"What do you think they do? Dispense penny sweets?"

"But two thousand, five hundred?"

Martin viewed the young man before him with an avuncular grin. "You've got to speculate to accumulate in this world, Steve, my old son ..."

SEVEN

It was Buzz's birthday and they were on their way to the coast. Anita, Buzz and Mel were seated in the back, with Anita placed behind Steve, who was sitting in the passenger seat. Every now and then she leant forward and prodded at his back, and their fingertips met, a private duel of sorts. The interior of the car was hot, oppressively so; a miniature, scented Christmas tree, deep green like Vinnie's leaf, swung from the rear-view mirror, compounding the air of claustrophobia. Buzz's father's taxi badge was still affixed to the dashboard: the image had him with his head tilted to one side, chin down, a look of "try it if you want to" in his dull eyes. It was hard to keep the thumbnail photograph out of your line of vision; the fact that it was the size of a postage stamp made little odds. They had stopped at a set of traffic lights on the A64.

"Don't you just love the shape of that new Jag?" Buzz's father said, indicating the car alongside which they had pulled up. To Steve it was just another large, snub-nosed vehicle. The driver had the window down an inch and every so often a wisp of cigarette smoke was sucked out into the atmosphere.

"Wouldn't do many miles to the gallon though," Steve replied, really in order to say something.

Buzz's father did not respond at first. He continued to look straight ahead, but appeared to be considering Steve's remark. "Don't think he gives a toss," he finally opined.

They set off again and for a moment it looked as if Buzz's father was trying to keep up with the Jaguar: something in the windscreen area began to rattle.

"Shurrup," Buzz's father hissed, smacking the dash where it said *Airbag* with the flat of his hand. The vibration stopped.

The Vale of York flashed past, field after field, hedge after hedge. The uniformity of this arable plain, each square metre spoken for, had a lulling effect. Through heavy eyes Steve's thoughts – as they had done countless times over the past forty-eight hours – returned to The Oval. Later that fateful night, after Mary-Anne had turned in, Martin and he had watched *Today at The Test*. They had shown some of the strokes that had gone to make up Levine's century. Martin's enthusiasm had been touching: he had watched each shot as if he were watching the game live, willing England on, willing on Steve's bet to conversion. But reflecting on it now, as the fields of stubble raced past in a haze of gold, what was extraordinary was how the result seemed in a manner preordained. It was as if Steve's bet had actually influenced Levine, or that was how Steve could view it – if he chose to. Of course there was little logic in this: he had merely taken a bet on a sportsman's performance; but watching the innings grow in its methodical fashion, reliving the unfolding strokes, one after the other, it was not difficult to believe that he had had some involvement, some strange complicity in the outcome. That or he had been given prior notice of the game's result. This, too, was an attractive hypothesis, one that put a spring in your step. A hotline to chance: it was like the man who has the ability to dream the lottery numbers before they are selected.

They stopped to fill up with diesel. All five disembarked. A fresh breeze blew their hair over their foreheads and into their eyes. You could just smell the sea from here; the effect was to make the city streets recede further than the forty odd miles they had hitherto travelled. Anita was all over Steve. One moment she was climbing on his shoulders, like a child forcing an adult to give them a piggyback; the next she was standing square before him, staring into his eyes, pouting. Just before they set off for the final stretch to the coast, Steve found himself alone in the gents' toilet with Buzz's father.

"Get your leg over yet?" Buzz's father asked from the urinal.

Steve was at a loss.

"I'll take that as a no, then. But a word of advice: I wouldn't leave it too long, a girl like that wants pinning down, if you take my meaning."

Steve managed to swap seats with Buzz for the remainder of the journey. It was warm sitting between the two girls: he could feel their bodies yield into his own as they began their descent to the sea by means of a series of hairpin bends. Mel was better for knowing, Steve had decided. He had even come around to her Goth appearance: today her black top revealed more cleavage than usual, white breasts with blue veins like crazy paving. A success of this magnitude on the cricket made you feel as if you were walking on air. Like Robin Fellowes with his *add to basket* analogy, it was now almost as if Steve could point his cursor at either of these girls, go between them both as you might in a computer game. But these were private reflections of course ...

They parked up two streets back from the front, and made their way to the nearest off-license.

"Wait here," Buzz's father ordered.

He reappeared some minutes later, holding two plastic bags. There was an ice-cold six-pack of Castlemaine XXXX in one and two bottles of Blackthorn cider in the other. "If my father had done this for me when I was your age I would have been well impressed," he said, handing both bags to Buzz. "I'll be in *The Engine* if you want me," he finished, gesturing towards the end of the street. "No scrapping, all right? I've been on nights all week: I'm not in the mood for any heroics. I just want a bit of peace and quiet." And he was off.

The four made their way to the harbour. A smell of salt and fish greeted you with its full force only as you rounded that final corner, as if the first line of houses had done their utmost to preserve the surprise of the North Sea. The harbour front was crowded with day-trippers. Buzz and Mel advanced to the railings, directly below which a collection of fishing boats had been tethered to a wall blackened with kelp and barnacles. A hundred seagulls wheeled overhead, those on the point of pitching on the boats resembling the birds in the Hitchcock movie, feet forward, beaks hooked and screaming.

"Let's go to the beach," Buzz suggested, pushing away from the railings and turning right. Yet immediately he had dodged into an amusement arcade. The others followed into the darkened interior, everywhere flashing lights and flickering screens. Buzz made his way to a driving game and was at once seated before a mountain road of trees and icy bends. Mel chose a skiing game, again a snow-clad scene of advancing perils. Steve and Anita began to feed twopence pieces in the Penny Falls.

"This one, this one," Anita pointed, indicating a shelf where a bank of coins was cantilevered impossibly over the chasm below. As Steve began to feed in the coins, she hooked an arm around his neck, her right breast touching his shoulder, her breath on his cheek. Briefly he recalled Helena, her white teeth flashing in the afternoon sun, in a similar attitude as she had stretched to snatch Robin's letter; but the reflection was short-lived: a fault had at last opened in the coins, bringing a handful crashing into the steel tray below.

"All mine," Anita whispered.

Steve had enjoyed this game as a child. It had nothing to do with winning: it was more the sight of those hydraulic rams ceaselessly shoving the pennies into hopeless positions and the smell and stain of coins on your hands. That had been enough then. Now there was an added attraction. It was not so much that he was going to get rich playing this kiddies' game with its glowing picture of a waterfall emblazoned on the steel canopy at eye level. It was more a question of: could he beat the machine? Had he the skill to take the upper hand? And all the while ceaseless pop:

> *Ooh aah, just a little bit*
> *Ooh aah, a little bit more*
> *Ooh aah, just a little bit*
> *I'll give you love you can't ignore*

They moved on to the fruit machines. Steve had little experience of these; it was Anita who could show him which emblems were worth holding, how to work the nudge. She looked impressed by the mint, folded-exactly-in-half twenty-pound notes (Steve had brought sixty pounds of the winnings Martin had collected for him) as he separated one from the others for her to fetch change. Almost at once the machine began belching money.

"Easy when you know how."

But Steve soon tired of the machines: he had not the patience to learn or understand the elaborate and torturous rules, different for each. He lost ten pounds just like that and resented it. Anita managed to stop whilst ahead, and she funneled twelve pounds into her trouser pocket. Now that it had been effectively laundered through the machinations of chance, it was no longer Steve's, it was hers.

Shielding their eyes against the sun, they joined the line of tourists outside once more, heading out of town.

"I've got a pretty good idea where we are," Buzz said. "Follow me."

They were soon at the harbour's end. Ahead a pier stretched a limb of granite out into the crashing surf; to the left a broad incline led down to the beach. They bought some chips at the last chippie and made their way along the sand, away from the crowds of visitors who appeared to have reached the beach, and stopped, producing a bottleneck of sorts. Presently they were almost alone, with steep cliffs behind and just a vast expanse of grey sea before them. They sat, all facing the flat horizon, and opened a beer each.

"There must be some brass to be made here," Buzz said.

"Shut up about your money, Buzz," Mel admonished him. "It's right boring."

"There's that many visitors. Did you see the price of them hot dogs?"

"Tell him to shut up, Steve."

"Buzz, shut up."

It was not long before the cans of beer were pushed upright into the sand, allowing them all the freedom of both hands. Buzz lay on top of Mel as was his wont; Steve and Anita lay side by side, the sand giving to produce a bespoke mattress. Anita's lips were gentle and soft; there seemed no need for the rough kissing which was Buzz's speciality. There were four inches of Anita's waist showing; Steve ran his hand over the satin skin, and on to her hips, the denim also surprisingly soft. Once more he pictured Helena, her marble teeth, her bunched ponytails, her brown eyes. And considered how only weeks before he had not really fancied Anita, had not considered her as a partner. Now he was smitten ... apparently. It just showed how wrong you could be: how sometimes you need to try something in order to learn of its true essence. He would try everything now, he resolved. The door to the shop was hanging open; beyond myriad pleasures awaited him. Just click the mouse! As he played with the metal button of Anita's jeans, where her flesh bulged just proud of the waistband, the advice of Buzz's father came back to him. It was as if Anita could hear the words ringing in Steve's mind.

"Don't get any funny ideas. I'm keeping myself, you know," she whispered, "but you can touch me if you like."

Forty minutes later, satiated, they pulled apart. The sun was hot now, burning down through a cloudless sky. The breeze had abated too. Anita removed her top and lay, eyes closed, on her back, her bra a brilliant white against her coffee-coloured skin.

Mel was on her feet. "I'm going to get some water," she said.

"There's cider here," Buzz offered.

Mel shook her head. "Want anything anyone?"

"I'll come too," Steve said, kissing Anita a final time and standing.

They walked in silence for fifty metres, before Mel said: "Anita's really into you, you know."

"I know," Steve replied, immodest.

"I thought maybe once she'd got you she'd lose interest ..."

"Thanks, Mel."

"You know what I'm saying? It won't be like that for you, will it? I mean, Anita: she's special."

"I know."

"Because it was Helena you were into, wasn't it?"

Under Mel's scrutiny, Steve looked out to sea. In the very far distance a fishing vessel supported itself on the silver horizon. "That's changed now," he answered with some conviction.

They reached the pier and proceeded to the shops beyond. It now became apparent that Mel wanted to make a phone call: rather than use someone's mobile she had walked those two hundred metres to reach a call box: she was that type of girl.

"I'll only be five minutes," she said.

Steve wandered some way up the pier to where a group of anglers were stood watching the tips of their rods. Then he sauntered back again. He seemed restless. He was not hungry, not thirsty – just restless. He began to make his way back up the pier once more, but almost immediately turned around. Now he was possessed of a new energy. He crossed the road and ducked beneath the doorway of a newsagent's shop. The interior was crowded, not only with people, but with items for sale which hung suspended from the low ceiling: lilos; buckets and spades; rubber rings; fishing tackle. He made his way to the counter.

"Two each of these, please," he said, indicating the scratch cards.

"Old enough are you?"

"Yep."

"Ten pounds."

Steve returned to the pier and sat on a bench carved from solid stone. He stared at the cards for a moment. With the latex intact you could invest these scratch cards with great power: each had the potential to make your heart skip a beat; the potential maybe to make you a rich man (actually the top prize money was seven thousand pounds on only one of the cards, *Buried Treasure*). Steve had played these lottery games once or twice before. He also knew that once the hidden emblems had been revealed to produce a losing combination these cards were just brightly printed pieces of cheap cardboard. It was "the not knowing" that was the magnet.

He began with *9 Lives* (keeping *Buried Treasure* for last). Here were three opportunities to win up to four thousand pounds, each line showing two latex black cats followed by a black circle with *prize* in white lettering. The numbers hidden beneath the two cats must add up to nine – then you would win the amount shown beneath *prize*. The first two cats revealed silhouettes of a cat's head complete with whiskers, with the numerals 3 and 5 printed in the centre. A loser. To delay starting on the second line, Steve scratched away at the encircled *prize*, to establish what he would have won – £3. No great shakes. He began on the second line. 2 and 5. Another loser, with this time potential prize money of £11. He did not hesitate to reveal the final numbers: 6 and 7. This time the latex prize revealed a sum of £999! Not bad if you'd been a winner, he acknowledged with a silent and slow nod of the head.

He studied *Pot of Gold*. Here was a treasure chest of grey and black, cleverly detailed to show its straps and a hanging padlock, with prize money of up to £6,000, and instructions: *Match 3 Like Amounts, Win That Amount*. The problem with this game was that there was really only one moment of anticipation, as all the numbers were concealed beneath the chest: try as you might, it was hard to reveal the numbers one at a time. Steve solved this by looking up at the sea as he scratched away on the surface of the cardboard. When he had finished he glanced down and read all the numbers simultaneously: £4, £37, £6,000, £100, £9, and £37. Nothing.

He turned his attention to *Holiday Bonanza*. This was a larger card with a bust of the Statue of Liberty as seen from below, shown to one side. This card boasted of *400 holidays worth £5,000 each to be won*. Again the object was to find three symbols – this time in a row, column or diagonal from the nine latex squares. And this time Steve was a winner! He had turned up three symbols of a blazing sun, with the word *sun* written beneath each. He drew a breath before scratching away the square that would indicate the prize money. £1.

Rabbit Riches was next. This game was more complicated, an inverse of the previous, it would appear. *Get 3 like amounts, win that amount;* or *Get 2 like amounts and win double that amount.* Presumably the game was geared to show no like amounts, or alternatively three like amounts with small prizes. Steve scratched the squares off one by one and to his amazement saw, as the field revealed itself, that he had two like amounts twice. There was £30 twice and £120 twice. He had won! He gazed at it anew. There was no mistake – he had won. And won handsomely: £120 twice. £240. He flipped the card over. Surely it would say that you won only the lesser amount. But there was no such stipulation. He looked up to the sea, his eyes settling on the far distance, where the grey, shimmering water met the horizon, barely discernible. His chest was heaving. Here he was, Steve Marsden, sixty eight miles (Buzz's father's computation) from home; he had gone into a newsagent's of his choice; and walked away with two hundred and forty pounds! He was charmed. The *It could be you* slogan of the National Lottery suggested itself to him. And he laughed aloud.

With renewed energy he tackled the *Buried Treasure* card. But there was something about the cartoon figure, with its metal detector and weird dancing worm top right, which warned him this card held no promise. He scratched away with his nail this time, to reveal an anchor, a key, a crown, two bones and a scroll. Nothing. But little matter.

Now that he had two hundred and forty-one pounds in the bank, so to speak, there seemed little need for any hesitancy with regard to removing the latex of the remaining five cards. He did so hurriedly and in the same order as he had tackled the first five. The *Pot of Gold* had two £3,000 amounts – that made him sit up – otherwise he drew a blank. He studied the winning card once more, removing the last vestiges of the latex, polishing it in his palm.

"What you doing?" It was Mel.

"What do you think I'm doing?"

"Won owt, have you?"

"Only two hundred and forty-one pounds."

"Have you chuff."

Steve proffered the *Rabbit Riches* with a grunt of satisfaction. Mel studied it carefully. Then she tossed it into his lap, top lip curled down.

"There's nothing on that."

"Whatdoyoumean? One hundred and twenty pounds twice, Mel. Two hundred and forty pounds. That's what it says."

"It says," Mel succinctly read, "'*Get 2 like amounts and* this'," she pointed now to what appeared to be a wad of cash, "'*and win double that amount*'."

Steve turned the card back and forth, over and over between his fingers. Mel was right. He had failed to take into account the wad of cash, so small, so badly drawn. It was a fraud! A complete and utter fraud!

"Bloody hell!" And there was a tremor in his voice.

"You shouldn't be playing those cards anyway."

"Spare me the lecture, Mel."

"You shouldn't, you know. There's shops round me where the streets are knee deep in these cards. There's kids that are going hungry 'cos their parents want to be a winner. It's not right."

"I can't help that, can I?"

"You can: by not playing them. They're bad, you know."

As they made their way back over the sand to join the others, Steve put a hand in his back pocket. There he felt the winning scratch card, all of one pound, and a note which he knew to be ten pounds. A day out at the seaside had cost him forty-nine pounds so far.

EIGHT

Rich's girlfriend, Sam, who had once worked for a graphic designer, had made a sign for the stall: *Edspinners*. The lettering was in red, gold and green. Bottom right there was a blobby arrow, pointing down at the "shop". Vinnie and Rich had managed to fix this well above the steel framework the council had afforded them. It was one of the first things you saw as you passed through the pillared entrance into the outdoor part of the market.

At first, Steve made good progress in negotiating the throng of people who crowded the fruit and veg area, but as he reached Vinnie's aisle he was brought up short. For ahead – and they could have been customers of *Edspinners* – were two police officers: one policeman, one policewoman. Both were in shirtsleeves, both wore their leather belts, a truncheon attached at one side, a pouch for handcuffs at the other. By their attitude and weighted gestures, Steve could see that they were not cautioning Vinnie, but he could also see that what was being said was being imparted with an air of firmness. The policewoman seemed to be fingering some of the pipes and paraphernalia; her male colleague was doing most of the talking. Then they turned as one, as if on a parade ground, and made their way towards the covered area.

"Trouble?" Steve asked as he reached the stall.

"Naaah," Vinnie winked, "just doing their job, aren't they?"

"Just like we're doing ours," Rich added.

"What were they saying?" Steve persisted.

"They didn't seem too impressed by the herbal ecstasy," Vinnie grinned. "They've told us to put it away pending some enquiries they're going to make."

"Herbal ecstasy!"

"Relax: it's organic, isn't it?"

"Christ, Vinnie; you're going to get into trouble."

"As if ..."

"They'll be watching you."

"I've got nothing to hide. You show me what's illegal here." And he waved a hand over the surface of the table.

New on display were items for which Vinnie had given the term *Classic Paraphernalia,* items from decades gone by. This mainly comprised steel plaques, the type you might screw to a bedroom door. One read *Stoned Again*; another *Keep On Trucking*; a third *Keep Off The Grass*. Each depicted a figure in caricature, face dissolving into his hands, or striding in midair. New, too, was a comprehensive range of cigarette papers of every colour, size and composition, along with neat stacks of brass-coloured gauzes, presumably for the pipes.

"Have you sold much?" Steve questioned.

"You have your touches," Vinnie replied. "Should have been doing this for years, you know," he finished with real conviction.

Steve took a chair and sat to one side of the stall.

The market had a vibrant atmosphere. If you closed your eyes the continual murmur of voices and the bustle of toing and froing resembled the passage of water in a beck. Over this there was the staccato *Six for a pound your Moroccan oranges* or *English strawberries: three for one pound fifty*, from the fruit and veg area outside the covered market. There was even a kiddies' merry-go-round, concealed behind the stall selling tape cassettes and posters, and every now and then the chime of a bell would ring out. He did not feel completely comfortable sitting alongside these pipes and this smoking equipment – it wasn't exactly his scene – but on a hot day like this, there could be no better place from which to watch the world go by. Here was an endless movement of people, people moving like ants, each invested with a sense of purpose.

But he was shortly to be shocked for the second time that day, for there, making a beeline for *Edspinners*, were the two men Steve had observed outside San Petino some weeks before: the stocky, dark-haired man, and his fairer accomplice. They came to a standstill directly in front of Steve's chair, but it was Rich the dark man addressed.

"Think you're funny, do you?"

Rich exchanged glances with Vinnie. "Hear a joke, did you?"

" ...Bringing the coppers in here – like flies to shit."

"What are you calling shit?"

"There's enough coppers in here anyway without you lot waving a flag. Friends of yours, are they?"

"Not friends of yours, it's obvious."

The fairer man joined his mate in front of the stall.

"You want to watch yourself, clever prat," the first went on.

Rich straightened. "Don't start thinking you can push your weight around here," he said.

"Why don't you piss off to the arcade?"

"I'll tell you why: because we're stopping here."

When they had gone, Steve found that he was trembling. Vinnie, too, looked shaken; but Rich was steely-eyed: the exchange had angered him.

"I've seen them in town," Steve volunteered.

"And I've seen them in here, and many more like them. They're just smack-heads."

"What?"

"Junkies: they go around the market thieving to pay for their drugs – scum! The more coppers the better for the likes of them."

Those two men, with their pasty skin and dull eyes, had filled Steve with a sense of foreboding. "Why *don't* you take a stall in the arcade?" he frowned.

"We might come the winter. But we're doing fine here just now."

Vinnie began to rearrange the pipes over the yard of cloth used to conceal the bare boards of the council's trestle, lining them up in columns, placing one in front of another. He looked perturbed, uneasy, a shadow of his former, cocky self. His tinkering with the goods seemed to be a way of calming himself and disguising his feelings. Rich, by contrast, stood stock-still; then suddenly he was off – he wanted to follow the two men into the market proper, to discover where they congregated.

"But *this* is all drugs," Steve said after some minutes silence, perhaps unconsciously taking advantage of his brother's moment of vulnerability.

"Eh?"

"It's double standards: you're selling this stuff on the one hand and you're criticising them," he waved in the direction of the covered market, "on the other."

"We're not *selling* drugs, Steve."

"But you're selling the stuff that goes with it."

"There's a difference."

"I know: but it's still all drugs."

"Anyway, since when did people rob for a draw?" Vinnie asked. "That's the difference: they're into hard drugs; this stuff is for soft drugs."

"It's still drugs."

Vinnie was more animated now. "And there's two hundred pubs in this town. What are they selling: pop?"

There was a seam of truth in this. "But the pubs have a licence," Steve objected.

"So?"

"So they're acting within the law."

"The law on dope's going to be changed soon," Vinnie stated.

"Oh yeah? Who said so?"

"Just about everywhere in Europe they have cafés where you can smoke."

"And they say that soft drugs lead to hard drugs. This stuff," Steve went on, indicating Vinnie's wares, "gives you them," he finished waving in the direction of the covered market.

"That's rubbish, that is."

"That's what they say."

"Listen, Steve: there's over three million people in this country who enjoy a smoke. They don't fight, they don't make a nuisance of themselves – they just go about their business. The horse has bolted – there's no locking any doors now. There isn't anyone who can turn back the clock as far as this is concerned. The sooner they come to accept that fact the better. For the likes of them ... there's going to have to be some other solution. But I can go to sleep at night doing what I do, and, as far as I'm concerned, that's what's important."

There had been more conviction in Vinnie's words and there was logic in his reasoning. Steve sank into silence, Vinnie's music underlying his thoughts.

> *We'll be together with a roof right over our heads*
> *We'll share the shelter of my single bed*
> *We'll share the same room, oh, Jah provide the bread ...*

ক

"They've got it so soon?"

"Next week they get the keys."

"Really?"

It would have been hard not to be up to speed on the minutiae of the purchase of Flat 4, 8 Sycamore Drive, since this was pretty much the only topic of conversation in the house at present.

"There is a lawyer who has just bought the top floor flat," Steve explained to Mrs Holland, "and he'd had a survey done and all that kind of thing. He sold it on to Martin for half-price. That saved them quite a lot of time."

"Good for them. And a lawyer will have looked into all the leases, I suppose," the old lady nodded. "That's a good thing."

"As soon as they get the keys Martin is going to *'take it to pieces'* – or that's how he puts it anyway."

"You might take me some photos so I can see?"

"Of course I will."

"I can't really imagine it."

So Steve described the shuttered front room; the back room overlooking a garden (and the possibility of knocking the two through to make one open plan living area); the galley kitchen; the rather dark and gloomy hall. He even mentioned the *Festival of Britain* style wallpaper in the bathroom's airing cupboard.

"I'm not sure I know the Sycamores," Mrs Holland then said. "Is that a good part of Marston Hill?"

"Excellent," Steve enthused. "It's walking distance from the centre; a lot of people coming up from London have been buying there apparently."

"London? My!"

"A flat came on the market last week, you know a flat ready to move into: and it was sold in two days."

"Heavens!"

It seemed that Mrs Holland must now digest this wealth of information. She leant back on her pillows and closed her eyes. There was nothing unusual in this: quite often she would doze unselfconsciously in the presence of visitors. Steve turned in his seat to face the lawn beyond the old lady's window. There were no birds hunting for worms today, since many of the other residents, seated in a semicircle of garden chairs, were enjoying the sun. A plane inched across the cloudless sky, depositing a stain of vapour in its wake.

If he *were* to win the lottery, Steve was thinking, how would he react? On seeing the numbers tally one after another, would he stand up and let the world know at once? Or would he take his time to grow accustomed to these new riches; perhaps take even a fortnight getting used to the fact before making his claim – after all, it said on the back of the ticket that you had one hundred and eighty seven days to "notify the National Lottery of your intention to make a claim". Intention to make a claim! He silently decided that he would in all likelihood wait a while in order to be ahead of the pack, since, a rich man now, there would be demands on him. Perhaps "demands" was the wrong word. But there would be people whom he would want to help. Who? His mother first and foremost: they could now afford any property that took their fancy. Then Martin: he could set him up in business properly, perhaps even take a lease on a shop from which he could run his operations. And Vinnie: again a shop. Anita: any amount of clothing and accessories. Helena? No, under the circumstances it would be too embarrassing to offer Helena anything. But perhaps a donation to an institution or movement whose aim was to safeguard the environment would be in order. Yes, he would definitely need time to decide how to cut the cake, how much to bestow on whom, without the world watching his every move.

"And Vinnie," Mrs Holland then said, easing out of her reverie. "I've heard about Vinnie's stall from Mary-Anne. I do hope I've done the right thing giving him that money. I feel rather responsible."

"It's all above board," Steve tried to reassure her, at the same instant picturing the police officers in the market. "There are stalls and shops like his all over the country."

"I mean, as far as I'm concerned," Mrs Holland went on, apparently ignoring Steve's comments, "money is a kind of energy. Of course sitting in a bank account it does nothing at all. But put to a use – then it becomes a facilitator. It's where that energy is directed which is the all-important question. What a lot of nonsense you must think I'm talking."

"Not at all," Steve responded genuinely, at the same time thinking that this line of reasoning sounded better coming from Mrs Holland than it did coming from Robin Fellowes.

"And I'm not a judge who can say which cause is worthier than another. How would I know anyway? It is up to the individual's conscience."

"Vinnie's conscience is quite clear: he told me so."

"I should hope so too. There is nothing worse than doing something against your better judgement. Your father would have been the first person to agree with me there."

"And he's doing nothing illegal."

Mrs Holland turned to fix Steve with her clear, grey eyes. "No, I don't suppose he is. But there are still legal things that aren't so ... savoury. There has been quite a row with the tobacco companies lately, hasn't there?"

Steve did not answer.

"Anyway," Mrs Holland finished, "it really isn't for me to say. Naturally I would be upset if Mary-Anne were upset ..."

"I think secretly she's rather proud of what Vinnie's done," Steve said, half-telling the truth.

"Is she?" Mrs Holland rhetorically asked.

They sank into silence once more. The sun had moved behind the oak tree, casting a broad shadow over the lawn. Steve could see a discussion taking place amongst the residents: they were evidently planning to come inside.

"I had rather a stroke of luck the other day," he spontaneously volunteered.

"Oh?"

"You remember Levine's century at The Oval? I had a tenner on that at twenty-to-one."

As soon as he had finished speaking he wished he had never opened his mouth. But his words hung in the air, like a scent, impossible to ignore.

"You didn't?" Mrs Holland breathed, turning quickly to face

him. "You had a bet?"

"Just a small one."

"I wish you hadn't told me that!"

"But I won two hundred quid ..."

"Steven, gambling is a vice."

"I know ..." the young man stuttered, hopelessly back-pedalling, but there did not seem to be any room for manoeuvre. "I know. I don't know how it happened. It just did."

"Only ruin comes of gambling. Mark my words."

A different type of silence now reigned. Steve felt utterly deflated. That he had won Mrs Holland's disapproval was a matter of real and immediate concern to him. The residents were coming inside now, with the nurses in tow, and the sound of their voices began to fill the corridor. He glanced imploringly at the old lady – but her face was turned away.

He would never bet again, he swore to himself – knowing in his heart that this was an unrealistic resolution.

NINE

The plaster had been removed from the internal wall of Anita's kitchen to reveal bare brick. This whole had then been varnished. The clot red of the terracotta clay seemed to glow with an intensity that told of a hidden power: it could be that they were underground in a hermit's grotto, or deep within the great mass of stone of an ancient pyramid.

Anita and Steve were seated with their backs to the wall on a trestle bench. Raff, Anita's mother, was preparing a round of sandwiches at the work surface beneath the window. Although the day was warm she wore a cardigan. In the pocket, ungainly and stretched, she had pushed the telephone, the receiver of which was wedged between her collarbone and cheek. The telephone had a seemingly endless extension chord, which enabled her to move around the kitchen at will; indeed she could even open the front door without interrupting her conversation: Steve had seen her do it. She spoke more than she listened. There was no problem in eavesdropping: these were not private calls as such.

"And why am I getting the name Christopher?" Raff was asking as she reached for a jar of peanut butter. "And John and Jack? Are they still with us or have they passed on? Yes, yes. Well, I can tell you now that John says you're going to make this work, you're going to be okay. But he says you've got to have confidence in yourself, go with your instincts: if you listen to other people and let them sow seeds of doubt, well ... it's going to make things that much harder. Because there are people out there who don't want us to succeed, aren't there? Do you know what I mean? Is that okay?

Because John says you've got it in you – he wants you to know that everything *will* be okay, but he's also saying that if you stay true to yourself, things are going to happen that much quicker."

Anita was peeling an apple. She was trying to do it in one. Maybe then she would throw it over her shoulder and turn to view the person she would marry, Steve fleetingly thought; for listening to Raff dispense advice to these anonymous callers, it seemed that anything was possible now. Anita, who was of course familiar with these psychic readings, looked bored. Steve, on the other hand, sat staring at Raff's sandalled feet and the trembling telephone extension line, as if this in some way might improve his hearing.

"And I'm seeing a house now, or spaces," Raff went on. "Are you thinking of moving? Well, don't discount that possibility if it arises because I can see ... well, it's bigger than a cottage, because it looks like quite a large country house with a hill behind it with trees. Yes, I am definitely getting the countryside. You want to live in the country but feel you can't get there yet? You may get there sooner than you think: okay?"

Anita had at first been reluctant to explain her mother's profession (Anita's father had a new, young family in Leicester – thus her mother was, by default, the breadwinner). But lying on the bed upstairs, they could hear Raff talking and talking in the kitchen. It had aroused Steve's curiosity to such an extent that he had almost been alarmed by the nature of the conversations. It was then that Anita had showed him an advertisement in the back of a copy of *Marie Claire*. There was a line drawing of an open window, a candle on the sill, a moon beyond, with a dog or a wolf barking or baying beneath its milky glow. Lettering top and bottom read: *Psychic Connections – Astonishing – Accurate – Amazing. £1.50 per minute. Ring 0800 256478.*

This was how it worked. If you, a member of the public, wanted a reading with a trained and gifted psychic, you rang the switchboard on the 0800 number: they took your details – Visa number, home address, date of birth etc – then phoned you back with the telephone number of the psychic on duty at that moment in time. Readings were generally twenty minutes long, but extensions could be paid for by the minute pro rata. At the end of the month Raff would get a printout of all the readings she had given over the previous four weeks and a cheque. She received forty-five pence per minute and *Psychic Connections* one hundred and five pence.

"Don't people ring back and try to cut out *Psychic Connections*?" was the first question Steve asked.

"What do you mean?"

"If they've got your mother's number, why don't they get a reading from her direct for less that one pound fifty per minute?"

"Because my mother hasn't got a Visa swipe machine, has she?" Anita answered simply. "Anyway," she went on, grinning now, "that's bad karma, isn't it?"

"And she can make a living doing this?"

"She does private readings too: twenty pounds each. This is just bread and butter."

Raff was winding up now: "I've got John again. Now he's with someone ... is it Fred or Frank? Frank then. Yes, yes. And Frank is saying ... well, he's just agreeing with John really. He's saying 'be true to yourself, don't listen to the detractors, go out and be yourself, enjoy yourself and rest assured that at the end of the day, on the day of reckoning, you will be able to look back and see that things *did* turn out right: everything *was* okay'. There's nothing to worry about, love: you can take it as read. Goodbye."

Raff took the telephone from her cardigan pocket, replaced the receiver, and then joined them at the table. She placed the sandwich before her. She looked weary. She did not bite into the sandwich: rather she tore a corner from the square. This she held before her mouth as she ate. She fixed Steve with clear, hazel-green eyes.

"So: you're Steve?"

Steve found that he could not keep her gaze. "Yes," he answered.

"You two in the same class?"

"Yes."

Now Raff seemed to tilt her head back as she continued to study Steve. Again he found his eyes could not hold hers. Was it possible that she was reading his mind, he wondered? Could she see that his feelings towards Anita were ambivalent? That, by virtue of the fact that Helena still held a place in his heart, he was acting dishonestly, leading her daughter on a path destined for nowhere? Could she predict the future, he then asked of himself? Could she "see" the conclusion of his relationship with Anita, and the ignominy of his disgrace?

"You two want something to eat?" Raff offered.

"We're probably going into town," Anita replied.

"Tell Steve to make himself at home," Raff said, now studying her daughter. "Help yourself to something from the fridge if you're hungry, won't you, Steve?"

"Thanks."

Raff rose and returned to the worktop where she picked at some leaves from a salad bowl. There was genuine warmth in her hospitality, Steve thought, and he began to relax against the back of the bench, and glance about the kitchen. The window frames and shutters had been stripped of paint and polished with wax, complementing the bare, grained floorboards. This worked well with the exposed brickwork. Now the room did not feel subterranean and heavy as it had first appeared; rather, these natural, earthy materials lent the place a lightness and freshness. Even the sound of your voice had a natural resonance.

Raff returned to the table. She was still chewing. In one hand she held a pack of cards. She proffered the pack, now fanned, to Steve. "Take one," she said.

"Muum!" Anita objected.

Steve felt flattered by this gesture: flattered that he was the centre of attention.

"You don't have to if you don't want to ..." Anita persisted.

"What are they?" Steve asked.

"Tarot cards."

Steve made a show of indecision, then chose a card from the centre of the fan, the most nondescript, as he saw it, of the pack. He turned it over – to reveal The Fool. This card bore the image of a jester, a flower in one hand, a package tied Dick Whittington-style to a stick balanced over his shoulder held in the other, stepping over the edge of a green cliff into an abyss. A small black and white dog was snapping at his heels. The Fool wore a stupid, unknowing smile, as if he almost welcomed and embraced his hopeless destiny. Burning blood rose to Steve's cheeks and he flushed bright red.

Raff smiled sympathetically. "Could be worse," she laughed.

"What does it mean?" Steve stammered.

Raff fixed Steve with her hazel eyes. This time he returned her scrutiny. "The world would be a dull place without The Fool," she began. "Okay: The Fool is young and naïve but he is going out into the world – he is embracing life. The card suggests that there may be beginnings, and there may be risks ... elements of uncertainty and the unexpected in whatever opportunities are thrown your way. The fact that you've turned it over in reverse would suggest that you need to take a little more care: think before you act – no matter how attractive a proposition may appear to you. But as I said," she finished, "the world would be a dull place without The Fool. Everyone needs a bit of greenness and the joker in their life."

☙

Waste Master had painted their skips a day-glow green. You could see the one outside 8, Sycamore Drive streets away. As Steve approached he read the smaller writing: *ISO14001 approved: Gets Your Rubbish to the Right Destination Every Time.*

Descending to garden level by way of the four steps to the entrance of the flat, Steve could hear the sound of Martin singing within:

> *Something in the way she moves*
> *Attracts me like no other lover*

He pushed through the gloss-black door, which was a few inches ajar, stone and gravel scraping on the floor as it swung on its hinges. Curtains of dust hung within. Martin was in the back room.

It was amazing the amount of "damage" you could do in a few days. Where the plaster was shot (or "knackered", as Martin put it) he had hacked it off the wall and shoveled it into four mounds in each of the room's corners. What remained looked like the uneven contours of a map standing proud on the brickwork – brickwork which, in its present state, bore no resemblance to that he had just been admiring in Anita's house. The hearth had also been the object of Martin's attentions. Owners from years gone by had boxed this off with hardboard – now the hardboard had been prised apart enough to establish what lay behind. In its present state the whole fireplace area resembled a damaged biscuit tin, its lid crooked and askew.

"Alright, Lucky Jim?" Martin hailed his stepson.

"How's it going?"

"This is the kind of work you can do drunk," Martin replied, wiping his brow, which was white with plaster dust. "You've just got to go in there and *do the business* ..."

"You haven't got that much stuff in the skip yet."

"Cheeky!"

"How are you going to get all this rubbish up into the skip anyway?"

"Barrow it."

"Couldn't you hire a conveyor belt?"

"Conveyor belt, my arse."

Mary-Anne had insisted on viewing the flat the day before contracts were exchanged ("You've got your work cut out now, Martin, she had said, almost grimly). Otherwise no one had visited. For this reason Martin was eager to conduct a guided tour to show the progress he had made in just three days.

"I've already had one skip load out of here," he proudly announced, leading Steve into the kitchen, where all the appliances, worktop units and cupboards had been removed, each leaving a shadow in reverse, like a photographic negative, on the wall. The bathroom suite had been left in situ ("Pukka gear that; quite a demand for stuff like this," he had said) but the airing cupboard was gone. The *Festival of Britain* wallpaper now lay in shreds on the floor.

The carpet along the length of the hallway had been lifted, revealing shuttered concrete, and had been pulled roughly into the front room. The window shutters of this room were closed, a steel arm holding the concertina panels in place, and a thin light pervaded the whole. If this were Lilliput, the great mounds of hessian-backed pile could be mountain range, with unbridgeable chasms and valleys treacherously seducing you to proceed, leading you to a head where further progress would prove impossible.

Steve followed Martin back to the kitchen. By the window area he had positioned a table fashioned from the door of the old airing cupboard, simply supported by four beer crates. They sat at either end of this table on the two chairs inherited from the previous tenant of the flat. On the surface of the airing cupboard door was a kettle, Martin's tin of rolling tobacco and a copy of *The Daily Mirror*. The newspaper was open and folded on page 48, *Mirror Racing*.

If the truth be told – and Martin was certainly not party to this knowledge – Steve had already had a number of bets on the horses over the past fortnight. He had made his selections with Buzz sceptically looking on, and then given the money to Buzz's father. It was strange: almost as soon as the money left his hands he had known that it was lost. It was as if Buzz's father was bad luck (in fact he had suspected that Buzz's father had pocketed the cash without even visiting the bookie's). It had been disheartening. Of eight selections he had had one winner at nine-to-four; two short-priced seconds; the remainder had been "also-rans". He had lost somewhere in the region of forty pounds – actually sixty pounds if you were being completely honest. But he was still ahead, on account of Levine's and Davenport's phenomenal performances at The Oval. Now he picked up *The Mirror*. There were some grease stains bottom right and a smear of what looked like egg yolk as well – Martin had evidently been studying the cards over a café breakfast.

"Fancy your luck, do you?" Martin tittered.

"Martin: what's a yankee?"

"It's a series of bets, isn't it? In fact, eleven bets," the other automatically answered, leaning over a bucket of water in which two mugs were submerged. "A straightforward yankee is four selections: and out of that you get six doubles, four trebles, and a roll up. A ten pence win yankee costs you one pound and ten pence."

"A roll up?"

"An accumulator. If your four horses won," he explained, pointing at the columns of data, "you'd get the winnings from one going onto the next and next and so on. If they all won at ten-to-one on ten pence you'd be looking at a pound going onto ten-to-one, that's ten pounds going onto a ten-to-one, that's one hundred pounds onto ten-to-one: a grand."

"A *grand*?"

"Not so bad for ten pence, eh?"

Steve placed the newspaper on his lap and, as Martin began to make a cup of tea, scrutinised the dense blocks of print. Today's meetings were at Hamilton and Brighton. Racing between the two tracks was staggered by one quarter of an hour, presumably to afford punters the length and breadth of the country a window of fifteen minutes in which to make their next selections. For both meetings two tipsters – *Newsboy* and *Bouverie* – had made their own selections. Each had a horse beside which was written "(NAP)".

"Martin, what's NAP?"

"A banker. A sure-fire thing."

Steve found this amusing and laughed aloud. He hunted for *Bouverie's* NAP in the 2.45 pm at Brighton: *Illiterate*. But this horse was a five-to-two favourite. Who would want to bet twenty pence to win fifty?

"And what are all these numbers?" he then asked.

"You're going get me bloody shot ... Which numbers? Them? They tell you how the horse was placed in its last races ... This one, *Mountain Deep*, for instance, came nowhere, nowhere, second, third, and most recently: nowhere. A donkey."

"And these numbers?"

"Handicap: tells you what weight they're carrying. This one, *Safe Haven*, is carrying nine stone thirteen pounds," he explained, pointing to the top of the 2.15pm at Hamilton, "and this one at the bottom, *Horrid Henry*, is only carrying eight stone three. Day like today I back top weight, me."

"What do you mean, 'a day like today'."

"Going is only good, isn't it? Bit of mud around."

Steve frowned. There was much more to this than met the eye. He had won three hundred and twenty pounds on Davenport and Levine in part because he had an interest in cricket: had not he fancied their chances? As far as the horses were concerned he may as well close his eyes and pick his selections with a pin. This knowledge made him feel lost, as if he were at sea with featureless horizons on all sides – yet still he was determined to have a flutter.

As Martin methodically prepared them each a drink of tea – washing the mugs in one bucket, rinsing them in another – Steve continued to gaze at the page of newsprint before him, his focus softening, his eyes moving blindly about the tangle of data and statistics. His thoughts, too, began to lose their focus: now he was picturing Raff with her back to him as she spoke in her kitchen; he could hear her voice rising and falling with its gentle tones of persuasive conviction. Before long the Hamilton card was no more than a cauldron of names and numbers – but, for whatever reason, there were some names that seemed to demand more attention than others. *Little John* and *Mighty Pip*, for instance, stood out from the crowd; so did *Trailer Park* and *Mark Anthony*. Steve snapped out of his reverie. As he did so, the names of those horses which had previously seemed to warrant more attention than the others lost their boldness – no longer did they appear highlighted. With difficulty, Steve managed to let his eyes focus beyond the page once more and so return the card to its meaningless state, names repeated twice, numbers superimposed endlessly over each other. There was no doubt about it: *Trailer Park, Mark Anthony, Little John* and *Mighty Pip* burnt with an intensity which kept them well apart from the competition.

༒

"And as they make their way out into the country seven furlongs from home it's the pink colours of Maestro *in front with* Up For It *in second,* Sea Breeze *on the rails running in third ..."*

Steve was standing to the right of the door of the bookie's – to be more precise beneath the image of the goalie diving to his right. The interior of the shop was more crowded today, perhaps on account of it being earlier in the afternoon: this was the 2.15 at Brighton.

"As they race towards the four furlong marker it's Sea Breeze *coming to the front now with* Up For It *in second,* Maestro *and* Negative Man *third and fourth ...* Mark Anthony *beginning to make a move ..."*

The television showing the video link of the race was positioned above the door, out of sight to the street. The eyes of all the punters within, who were leaning against counters which ran the length of the walls, were lifted to the ceiling – as if this were a church. If Steve tried hard enough, he could just make out the progress of the race reflected in a sheet of glass at the far end of the shop upon which was written in bold letters: BET HERE. But hearing the name of his horse he bowed his head and focused on the pavement beneath his feet.

"Turning now for home, three furlongs out, as they begin to wind up the pace it's Sea Breeze *from* Maestro, Negative Man *and* Mark Anthony: *they're all in contention …It's* Sea Breeze *from* Negative Man *and* Mark Anthony: *they're running in a wave …"*

Once again Steve noticed how the inside of the shop had come alive. No longer were punters free to prop themselves against the counters of veneer: now they must circulate within the four walls, like fish trapped in a pool.

"It's Negative Man *and* Mark Anthony *who go on,* Sea Breeze *can't go with them …"*

The commentator's voice reached a new pitch of intensity and anticipation.

"As they hit the final furlong marker it's Mark Anthony *who has it from* Negative Man *under pressure. They're clear of the field. It's* Mark Anthony *by a head from* Negative Man *… with* Cincinnati *now coming through on the rails. It's* Mark Anthony *from* Cincinnati *racing in second. It's* Mark Anthony *from* Cincinnati *… Up towards the line … number six,* Mark Anthony *has it, second number twelve,* Cincinnati, *photo for third."*

There was a sour taste in Steve's mouth, a taste of iron. Some punters were coming out of the shop now. As they did so, their eyes screwed up against the street's brightness, they tossed their losing betting receipts to the floor. If the world were a kinder place Steve would stop one of them to show them the names *Little John* and *Mark Anthony* written at the head of his yankee. He now had two out of four.

"Result of the 2.15 at Brighton: first, number six, Mark Anthony 8-1; second, number twelve, Cincinnati, seven-to-two joint favourite ..."

Steve made his way back to Sycamore Drive. As he did so, he studied the pink carbon copy of his betting receipt. He resembled a student making final revisions for an exam. He had eventually managed to persuade Martin to place a one pound win yankee, costing eleven pounds, in favour of the other's preferred ten pence bet. *Little John* had won at four-to-one. There was therefore five pounds (winnings plus stake) going onto *Mark Anthony* at eight-to-one. The bet was now worth forty quid. Another winner and he would be in the money; another two winners ... It seemed that Steve must breathe hard to keep control of his thoughts, to feel the ground beneath his feet.

Martin made a point of not sharing his stepson's enthusiasm. "Don't go counting your chickens," he shrugged. "Come and see me when you've got three out of four."

But as three o'clock approached – Steve's next selection, *Mighty Pip*, was running in the three o'clock at Hamilton – Martin's curiosity had got the better of him. "You can use the phone if you like."

"What do you mean?"

Martin proffered *The Mirror* and his mobile phone. "Here: Racing Results. Use the 60p-a-minute number: I do it often enough."

Steve had intended to return to the doorway of the bookies to follow the race; that way Martin would not see his look of desolation should *Mighty Pip* fail to continue where *Mark Anthony* had left off. But it was raining hard now. Besides, wasn't Martin in some manner lucky? He waited until four minutes past three – "They've got to be punctual, they've got the whole flaming country waiting on them," Martin had told him – and then rang the 0906 number.

Charging at 60p a minute this company operated within its own timescale. Steve found he must listen to the results of the 1.30, the 2 o'clock, and the 2.30. Not only were second, third and, in some cases, fourth places given and the starting price of each, there was also other superfluous information: forecasts, tricasts, Tote. Finally the voice promised the information Steve sought: *"Result of the three o'clock Hamilton ... first, number twelve,* Mighty Pip, *six-to-one; second,* Highland Fling, *six-to-four joint favourite; third,* Les Miserables, *seven-to-two. Eighteen ran."*

"Martin, I've done it."

"You bloody haven't?"

"First, number twelve, *Mighty Pip* at six-to-one ..."

"You're the bloody Shining, you."

"Six-to-one!"

"Show me your bet ..."

Martin studied the betting receipt, an expression of dull concentration in his eyes, as if now he were the student. Steve joined him at his elbow. There was no mistake. One after the other these selections had come up: one, two, three. There were forces at work here: there was no question about it.

"How the hell did you manage that?" Martin asked.

Steve would of course not betray the manner in which he had sourced the names *Trailer Park, Mark Anthony,* and *Mighty Pip*. "I just fancied them," he answered simply.

But now there was a problem. And they both knew it. For when Steve had shown Martin his list of intended bets some two hours before, Martin had shaken his head gravely, balking at *Little John*. "You may as well drive down Monkton Hill and throw your money out of the window."

"What do you mean?" Steve had demanded.

"Well, look at its form. Nowhere, nowhere, third, nowhere and nowhere. It's little wonder it's a thirty-three-to-one outsider: hasn't a snowflake's chance in hell."

"You sure?"

"That horse'll be pet food at the end of the season."

And so, on Martin's advice – there wasn't time to sit down and let the card swim out of focus – Steve had changed his initial selection to a horse called *Intrepide*. This filly had been placed in each of its last four races, it was also Newsboy's NAP. It seemed like a sensible alternative.

Now Martin and Steve exchanged silent glances: there was almost a look of pre-emptive apology in the older man's eyes.

"I'm going out to listen to this one," Steve quickly said, and left the flat.

He made his way purposefully back to the bookmaker's. The rain had eased somewhat, though a thin drizzle hung like a mist in the air. He found that he was hot: he pulled open his collar. He had forty pounds going on to a six-to-one chance: there was two hundred and forty in the bank on that bet alone. He also had won three doubles, at four-to-one and eight-to-one, four-to-one and six-to-one, eight-to-one and six-to-one. There was a fair bit of money there. It seemed his mind kept wandering, trying to anticipate *Intrepide* winning at, say, three-to-one (a modest forecast) – his four-horse accumulator would then be worth ... But he stopped himself short: it was bad luck to tempt fate in such a way. All the while he was pinching the betting receipt between thumb and forefinger, as if this pressure would in some way improve his chances.

And then, as he turned into Chancellor Road, head down, shoulders forward against the drizzle, he virtually collided with a young girl, who, too, was proceeding blindly through the rain. It was Helena.

"Helena!"

"Steve ..."

They studied one another for a number of long seconds. Helena's hair was wet, stuck to her forehead. She wore an anorak of mauve.

"How are you, Helena?"

"I'm okay. And you?"

"Fine ... And your father?"

Helena paused before answering. She seemed to want to "meet" his eyes. "He's okay. He's in remission. Thank you for asking."

"I'm pleased for you."

"And you? You okay? You look ... Are you alright?"

"I'm fine."

Steve was now staring at the pavement, at Helena's calf length, fur-lined boots, the suede toes of which were black with damp. She did have a propensity for wearing inappropriate clothing: Whacky Helena was what they called her at school. A thick, almost tangible silence quickly asserted itself. This was, of course, the opportunity Steve would otherwise have taken to ask Helena out, and he knew it. But this knowledge was clouded and distorted by his urgent need to get on.

"I'll see you around, then," Helena said, sensing Steve's preoccupation, yet there was no awkwardness in her voice this time.

"Yes, I'll see you around ..."

When Steve reached the bookmaker's it seemed by the manner in which the punters were streaming out into the street that they were evacuating the premises. Some guffawed, others laughed derisively, some were shaking their heads; but all appeared to be fleeing its embrace, as if now they really had had enough. The pavement was littered with losing betting slips.

"Bollocks to it," he heard one swear.

"Tosser!"

Steve had to fight his way to the door. By the diving goalie he heard the words he had been unconsciously dreading:

Result of the 3.15 Brighton ... first, number three, Little John, thirty-three-to-one ...

TEN

"I can't remember the last time we all had a Sunday meal together," Mary-Anne murmured, as she absently watched Martin carve the joint of beef they had both prepared for lunch. "Is it cooked enough?"

"This is going to put a bit of weight behind the hammer ..."

"You're not working later, are you?"

"Might do. That's the joy of being your own boss: come and go as you see fit."

"But don't go upsetting Mr Harris on the top floor ... He looks so fierce."

"Bark's worse than his bite."

"How can you tell?"

"Just can."

It was as if Steve had been on a beach, fishing from the waterline. He had cast a line into the foaming surf, waited, and seen the rod tip bend almost to breaking point. There had followed a duel like no other – the fish had gone this way, then that way; it had gone out to sea, it had thrashed around amongst the breakers; it had gone deep. But then the line had gone slack and the rod tip straight. The prize specimen was off, free once more to lose itself in the vast expanse of the silver ocean. The feelings of disbelief, regret and desolation this loss of contact had occasioned were quite unprecedented. Steve had had to wait at the end of the street for fifteen minutes to compose himself. In fact, Martin had gone out to find him, worried by his stepson's prolonged absence; and had discovered him staring stupidly at the jinxed betting receipt. "Come on, cock: you'll be okay in a minute ..."

" ... this time tomorrow I'll be landing," Vinnie was saying.

"But what do you *do* in Amsterdam?" Mary-Anne asked, and there was a note of irritation in her voice.

"I'll be staying with Erik this time. We're having a meeting with the mail order people on Tuesday ..."

And now, two days on, it was still impossible to think of anything else. Granted he had come away that afternoon with over four hundred pounds, but there was the "loss" of over ten thousand to come to terms with (the four-horse accumulator would have paid ten thousand, three hundred and ninety-five alone). Beyond this there was the bitter, acrid taste of being "let down", which seemed to pervade every cell of his being. It was as if he had been taken so far only to be abandoned: the fish had hooked itself in the knowledge that it would eventually come free.

"I never use mail order," Mary-Anne was dismissively saying. "You never know what you're getting."

As Martin handed him a plate of food, Steve snapped out of his reverie. His eyes came to focus consciously on the gold bracelet Vinnie had recently bought himself, the links so heavy that they had had to be flattened to allow movement. The precious metal shone a dull lustre against his brother's tanned wrist. Business can only have been brisk. Yet his thoughts were soon to continue their ceaseless movement. For once again, in exactly the same way as he had considered when reflecting on Levine's and Davenport's winning performances at The Oval, he had the impression that his choice of horses had in some manner influenced the outcome of those races at Hamilton and Brighton. But there was further territory to explore on this occasion. He had selected those names by psychic means: he had allowed them to present themselves for selection. Was this a demonstration that he really did have some form of communication with a dimension beyond the ordinary?

"I think this calls for a toast," Martin said, finally taking his seat.

They had treated themselves to an ice-cold bottle of Petit Chablis: Mr Farouq had lately begun stocking a selection of *fine wines* in his corner shop. Mary-Anne smiled uncertainly as her glass was primed.

"Here's to our new ventures," Martin beamed, raising his glass.

Mary-Anne raised hers and took a sip so small the wine barely wetted her lips.

"Come on, Mary-Anne, please relax."

"I just don't like to be ahead of myself, that's all. We're in no position to tempt fate."

"We're not tempting fate ..."

"I've never known a summer like it," she wearily returned. "I shall be surprised if I've even earned two hundred pounds this month. Tissons have gone; Cooke's are on short time. Haven't you noticed how the telephone's gone dead?"

"A good job we've got Sycamore Drive, then."

"The whole country seems on shut-down."

"Anyway," Martin continued, refusing to be silenced and gesturing at Vinnie's wrist with his fork, "there are some industries that are healthy enough."

Mary-Anne grimaced. "Is it an industry?"

"Certainly it is."

"It's the leisure industry, Mum," Vinnie provocatively volunteered.

"And the leisure industries are on the ascent ..." There was a triumphant weight to the pause in Martin's delivery. "Because people have finally realised that *man can't live by bread alone.*"

"They won't be saying that when the bread's gone and there's only a plateful of crumbs," Mary-Anne quietly rejoindered.

Martin gave up here, turning his attentions to his food. A silence reigned, broken only by the sound of Vinnie's bracelet clunking against the surface of the table.

And then there was Helena. What was that song Martin used to sing to himself? *"Blue eyes crying in the rain"*. But Helena hadn't been crying. The rain may have given the impression that there were tears, but in reality she had been perfectly composed. She hadn't gloated, yet she seemed able to hold his eyes in a manner that suggested she would not be hurt again. Here was another fish that had gone. And how he must have appeared to her!

Lunch over, Martin stumbled to the sofa on the pretext of reading the papers. Mary-Anne's mood had improved; now she pampered her partner, bringing a coffee to his side, perching on the cushions below his knee.

"Don't go back to work later, will you?" she said.

"Don't you worry: I've got no intention of going back."

"And sorry to have been so gloomy at lunch."

"The world's a stressful place."

Steve took the two flights of stairs to his bedroom. He did so taking the steps two at a time, springing noiselessly from one to the other on tiptoe. Once behind his door he slid the bolt's lock – again noiselessly. For he did not wish to be disturbed. Or he did not wish others to be aware of what he was doing.

The day before, he had logged on to casinocasino.com, a website lately advertised on national television. This he had done to stare at the race results of Brighton and Hamilton. These were crystal clear in Martin's *Mirror,* yet still he had had an inclination to see them again and again, as if the sight of *Mark Anthony* and *Mighty Pip* would in some way clear and forge the path by which they had been selected.

Steve was dumbstruck by the depth and scope of this site. On the left was a column of twenty-six sports – included were hurling, hockey, speedway, Gaelic football and cycling. Entering through any of these took you through reams of odds – expressed as fractions or decimals at the click of the mouse – and betting scenarios, culminating in a coupon with boxes headed *Unit Stake,* and a button below, *Bet Now*. He checked the horses in the site's indigo blue print, then navigated to *Arcade*. Here a caption boasted: *From backing near certainties at one-to-ten to shooting for the moon at forty thousand-to-one, every bet is catered for.* There was even a game called *Heads Up: Heads or Tails? It's even money every time!*

- Cash In
- Select Heads or Tails
- Choose Your Stake
- Press Play

Steve had then gone to *Casino*, where another caption boasted: *You're only three minutes away from playing, simply download now and enjoy.* And: *All payouts independently reviewed by PriceWaterhouseCooper*, whatever that meant. In fact Registration took less than one minute (Steve was a nimble typist): he chose the word "sushi" as his Username and Password. Once downloaded a window read: *You may wager for fun in "Practice Mode" or for real money in our "Online Mode"*. Steve would be unable to play for real money, as he did not have a credit card with which to buy what was termed *E-cash*. So he pressed the "Practice Mode" button.

Presently there was a roulette table before him on the screen, not as seen from one end, like a tennis court at Wimbledon, but as seen from the side and above. The wheel was to the left. The table – with its odd/even, black/red, 1-18/19-36 near side – stretched to bottom right. casinocasino started you off with five thousand pounds. You bet by simply dragging your stake – which you chose from £1, £5, £25, £100 or £500 counters – onto the table. When you pressed the gold *Spin* button the wheel began to rotate and the ball to tick, tick, tick over the slotted spokes. A voice would then announce the winning number and an invisible hand move the gavel to its rightful position on the cloth. If you had a counter on a winning square or on the boundary of a winning square (Steve had to go to *Help* to acquaint himself with the odds), the voice would say, *Player wins*, and a display read: *You won £200.00 GBP*, for instance.

Steve let his vision distort, moving the numbered squares out of focus.

☙

Steve and Anita had been shopping for jewellery too. Initially Steve had planned to buy himself the iPod, but after he had bought Anita her necklace, he had seemed, for whatever reason, to run out of steam. Anita was not religious, and there were certainly no religious motifs in her house, yet she had chosen a simple gold crucifix. "Sexy," she had said on the bus home as she played with the fine chain at her collarbone.

Now they were seated in Anita's kitchen, with Raff at the head of the table. Scattered between them were the materials that went into making dreamcatchers: wire hoops, tan-coloured leather, catgut, glass beads and feathers. Raff's friend, Angela, had ordered eight dreamcatchers for her shop in town, *Timeless Earth*. If they could make the eight in one sitting between them, then Raff would give Steve and Anita half of the forty pounds, which at five pounds each was the going rate.

"Five quid each," Anita scoffed. "They're twenty odd quid in the shop, you know."

"So?" her mother shrugged.

"Don't you think we should get ten?"

"Not if someone else is prepared to make them for five."

They had set up quite an effective procedure involving a clearly defined division of labour. It was Steve's job to cut the leather into strips "about the width of a thumbnail"; Anita would bind the metal hoops of twelve inches' diameter with the leather, making sure that no part of the metal remained visible. Raff would then do the difficult bit: create the spider's web from catgut, on each frame incorporating perhaps two brightly coloured glass beads. Finally Steve must tie two feathers of guinea fowl, each suspended by three inches of catgut, onto the bottom of the frame. There was an industrious air about the trio. Anita's fingers worked with quickness and dexterity: she had evidently been roped into doing this before. Raff appeared serious.

"Where's this leather from?" Steve asked, really to break the silence.

A faint smile broke over Raff's lips. "This stuff's from old leather jackets that Angela buys at the car boot."

"Very earthy," Anita snorted.

"And how do these catchers work?" Steve went on, wanting to laugh too, but restraining himself.

"You hang them over your bed," Raff explained, "and they catch the bad dreams but let the good ones through."

"I thought it was the other way round," Anita objected.

"No," her mother insisted, "the bad dreams get caught in the web and die at dawn's first light. These feathers should be eagle feathers," she went on, "because the American Indians used to think their souls lived in animals; and the eagle was prized above all others for its strength and for the freedom of its spirit. But we don't have many eagles in this country," she finished, quieter.

"It's all rubbish, isn't it?" Anita then said.

"What's all rubbish?" Raff murmured, not even looking up.

"Catching dreams ..."

"Have you ever tried using a dreamcatcher?" her mother asked, lifting the frame she was working on and staring through the random webbing.

"Well, no ..."

Raff wore her more serious expression. "Don't you think you had better try one before you go making judgements like that?"

"Works for you, does it?"

"Certainly."

Here Steve looked up. Raff's expression had softened, yet now her posture reminded him of a teacher's, or perhaps even Robin

Fellowes's at *Pennine Recycling*.

"If you go through life being cynical you're going to miss out on an awful lot," she said. "Okay, these things work by suggestion – you've got to believe in them for them to work – but people wouldn't be buying them if they didn't do anything. The American Indians wouldn't have made them and used them if they didn't work. Where all this stuff is concerned you have to listen very carefully: the spirits' world is an awfully quiet place."

Here Steve frowned.

"Anyway," Raff concluded, "look at what's round your neck all of a sudden."

"What do you mean?" Anita teased, pointing the crucifix at her mother as if she were a demon.

"What do you think that's doing for you?"

"That's different: it's sexy."

"It's a sort of fertility symbol, is it?"

Now Steve found he was flushing.

"No: it's funky," Anita laughed.

A bottleneck of sorts had formed at Raff's elbow: there were now six frames to be worked on.

"Come on, get your finger out," Anita goaded.

"Here, you do one," Raff said to her daughter. "Just keep it tight."

As Steve waited for the next catcher (he had already tied the feathers on to their three inches of gut in readiness), he absently fingered the pack of Tarot cards to his right. Beyond the dozen or so picture cards there appeared to be four suits: Cups, Pentacles, Swords and Wands. It was pretty much like a pack of ordinary playing cards, only the picture cards – The World, Judgement, The Moon, The Devil etc. – were extra. There was a beguiling simplicity to the images. The Sun card, for instance, bore an image of two young children seated before a burning sun, this a thickset face with rouged lips and golden eyes. Next to the children were three sunflowers, their stamens resembling the pupil of an eye. Strength showed a woman in a blue cloak wrestling with a lion: she appeared to be trying to prise open its mouth. Justice had another woman, this time in red, holding a sword in one hand and balancing a set of scales in another – nothing unusual here. The Emperor and The Empress had them both sitting in thrones, each holding a golden orb in the palm of their hands and displaying a Coat of Arms; the only difference between the two seemed to be that The Empress was seated beneath a fruit tree. Steve began to bring the images he preferred to the front, then place them on the table before him. The Moon he put down: he liked the reposing "man in the moon" motif with the dogs baying before the half-light (this a bit like the advertisement of Psychic Connections); in the foreground a crayfish was climbing out of a pond. He placed The Hermit next to it. This showed a cloaked man holding a lantern in one hand, a walking stick, a serpent wrapped around its length, in the other. Next to that The Hanged Man, a shocking image of a young man hanging upside down by one foot, his arms bound behind his back.

Steve looked up, aware of a silence that had seemingly crept up on him. He was right to be self-conscious, for both Anita and Raff were regarding him. Raff's eyes seemed a lighter green than before. They were depthless. It sounded corny, but you could say that the universe was in those eyes.

"Keep going," she said.

"I'm only having a look," Steve mumbled, placing the card he had in his hand on the tabletop. This was The Tower, and showed a fort-like building being struck by lightning. From the top storey two figures, a young woman and a young man, were in the process of diving headfirst towards the ground, arms ready to break their fall, legs akimbo. Flames rose and licked from each of the buildings' Gothic-style windows.

"That's one you definitely want to avoid," Raff smiled. "But, hey; you know what they say: there's a silver lining to every cloud."

ELEVEN

Steve and Martin were sitting in traffic at the bottom of Monkton Hill. Unusually they were listening to a regional radio station – Martin would normally only listen to Radio 4 in the car. A chatty, irritating voice enunciated the news stories deemed to be of interest to the thousands of people across West Yorkshire like themselves, held stationary in queuing traffic in slanting rain.

"And finally: the Halifax Building Society has announced a marked cooling off in the housing market. In fact, house prices remained static across the country in the last month, leading some to speculate that the unprecedented rise in property prices may be over for good. We are joined by Simon Holden of The Halifax. What's it all about, Simon?"

Now a young man came on; he could have had the proverbial plum in his mouth.

"I think people may be feeling the plateau has finally been reached. When they see that properties at the bottom of the ladder are outside the range of first time buyers, and then look to the global markets and see them in recession ... well, the vast majority of people would be trying to reduce their burden of debt rather than increase it."

"Sounds like he's had a good lunch," Martin muttered with a sour expression.

"So where's it all going to end?"

"Not an easy question to answer ..."

"But you're going to have a go anyway, aren't you?"

"... I can see property prices falling by as much as thirty percent. Yes I can. And not all at once and not across the board. I mean there are

reports that house prices have fallen by between ten and fifteen percent since the spring in the Southeast. Yet prices have held up in the North, especially the Northeast."

"That's something then ..."

"What's your advice, Simon?"

Martin punched the off button on the radio dial. "Shuddup."

Yet this exchange was enough to steal the wind out of Martin's sails. They took the steps down to the front door of 8, Sycamore Drive in silence. And once inside, a smell of plaster brought to the fore by the dampness, they wandered from room to room without speaking.

To give him his due, Martin had completely transformed the flat. Everything that was going to be cleared – including skirting boards, doorframes, all the shot plasterwork – had gone. He was a tidy worker (his words). "Keeping up to date with the rubbish" was almost an obsession with him, though Steve had heard much balking at the cost of the *Waste Master* skips. "One hundred and ten pounds a time. The government's environmental tax just means that people are going to live in squalor." The flat looked much larger for being empty. But still there was the question of opening up two living rooms to make one long, open plan area. And a decision must be made sooner rather than later, since Martin had already started replastering the outside walls. His plan was to move from the back of the house towards the street.

Steve made his way to the kitchen and sat at the makeshift table. It was siling it down now; rain danced from the patio area immediately outside the back door – in fact the shattered droplets of water danced so high that it could have been raining in reverse. He was calculating thirty percent of seventy-two thousand pounds. Approximately twenty-one thousand, five hundred. Subtract that from seventy-two thousand and you got fifty-one thousand. This was roughly what they had paid for the flat once legal fees and stamp duty had been taken into account. It had originally been the intention to spend between ten and eleven thousand pounds in renovating the property. Perhaps if Martin made some savings here – abandoned the French Windows or chose an inferior specification for the kitchen appliances – perhaps then they would not lose so much. Losing say seven or eight thousand would not be the end of the world (especially in view of the figures he had come so close to winning recently). But it seemed a bitter pill to swallow given the amount of effort that had gone into the project so far. He joined Martin in the front room.

"Do you really think the market's going to fall?" he asked.

"Do I chuff? There's been people predicting all sorts for months, for years ..."

"But he was saying that it's already fallen in the Southeast."

"And no wonder. Prices had gone mad there."

Steve was playing the devil's advocate. "Haven't they gone mad here?"

"Come on, Steve, don't depress me ..."

A silence reigned. Martin stepped forward and began knocking on the brickwork separating the two living rooms with the knuckles of both hands, just as he had done when they had first viewed the flat. There was no hollow sound here.

"I just don't know," he grimaced.

"What?"

"Well, there obviously will be what they like calling *an adjustment*," Martin began, with that same sour expression. "You know, prices can't keep going up forever. And that's what they're seeing in London at the moment. But things always happen a bit later up here. Fashions, fads, trends: all that kind of thing; it always takes time for it to catch on up here."

"So?"

"Well, I can't see the market collapsing tomorrow – not up in West Yorkshire I can't."

"We are very close to town in Sycamore Drive," Steve encouraged the other.

"Of course we are. And I think ... if we made this into one room, it would make the whole, whole difference. It would mean that someone, a yuppie type, would come in here and offer for it there and then."

To Steve there was a winning ring to the wildness that he could hear in Martin's words.

"But then again," Martin frowned, prevaricating, "maybe we should be *playing safe* – especially on the first project."

Now he had once again donned the deflated, depressed mantle he had worn when they had arrived at the flat that afternoon.

"Is it a question of *nothing ventured nothing gained*? Or is it a question of *playing safe*? I just don't know."

"I've got an idea," Steve suddenly said, moving to his stepfather's side. "We'll toss for it."

"What?"

Producing a fifty-pence piece from his pocket and holding it between thumb and forefinger, Steve repeated his extraordinary idea. "We'll toss for it."

"Don't be ridiculous ..."

"Why not? You can't make your mind up: there's reasons on both sides for doing and not doing it. Let the coin decide it." Now he had his thumb cocked beneath the piece of hexagonal nickel.

"You're mad," Martin admonished the other. "You can't go round making decisions like this on the toss of a coin."

And Martin seemed to ignore Steve, as if he was not giving any further consideration to the other's preposterous suggestion. He knocked at the wall again, his top lip tight over his teeth, all the while muttering to himself. "We probably should do it, you know. Probably should. It wouldn't cost much; it wouldn't take that long. Oh Goooddd, I'm not sure."

"Heads you do it, tails you don't," Steve insisted.

Martin made a show of laughing to himself. "You're mad, you

are."

Pause.

"But you've got a point, you know," he presently said. "I'll never make my mind up at this rate, never." He laughed again, but this time it was a different laugh, more of a snort. When he spoke afresh he sounded like someone Steve had heard from the doorway of the bookmaker's. "Go on then: heads ..."

"You sure?"

"Hurry up! Heads."

Steve tossed the coin. Though the rain had not abated and a dull light glowed within the room, the fifty-pence piece flashed silver as it turned in the air. Steve caught it cleanly and turned it over on the top of his hand. It read tails.

"Bollocks!" Martin swore.

"Tails you don't do it, then?" Steve pronounced with the air of a judge.

"Bollocks!"

"But you want to do it, don't you?" Steve asked, and he could have been the devil himself, such were his tone and manner.

Martin looked pathetic, like a dog disciplined. "Of course I want to do it."

"Best of three, then."

"Shuddup."

"Come on ..."

"Go on, then: heads again."

Steve spun the silver coin. It landed heads this time.

"And again," Steve sang.

"Heads a third time."

The coin landed heads.

༄

"Well, well, I had no idea it was so big," Mrs Holland was saying as she studied the pencil drawing that Martin had produced the night he had presented his business plan to Mary-Anne.

"We have taken some photographs, but they haven't come out very well."

"But at the moment it's two rooms, is it?"

"The wall's coming down next week."

"Heavens!"

Mrs Holland closed her eyes. In this attitude of complete repose she could have been dead, her body laid out by the undertakers, white fingers interleaved over her stomach, her paper eyelids closed like shutters. Steve was finding that, for the first time, he was awkward in this silence: now that he had made the mistake of owning up to his wager on the cricket, Mrs Holland was bound to refer to it later on in the course of his visit that afternoon. Indeed a part of him had been dreading this week's visit.

A sense of resentment needled him, so strong that it made him squirm in his seat. The one thousand, two hundred and fifty pounds had been given "no strings attached"; she had no right therefore to judge where he saw fit to invest it. Yes – so why didn't he just give the money back? He could afford to do this: didn't he have more than he had started out with? When it came to burying talents in the sand, his money had actually been multiplying. And why did he need her anyway? All she did was keep a channel open to his father. Wasn't it time that his father's memory was buried once and for all?

Steve frowned at the unreasonable nature of his thoughts. He must put his house in order with regard to Mrs Holland – he could not afford to lose her, yet this relationship could only be retrieved by floating a raft of lies. A rising sense of panic seemed to wash over him. Martin had spoken harsh words too. All at once he was isolated, alone.

Mrs Holland cleared her throat. But still she remained perfectly still, eyes closed.

Steve revisited the scene at Sycamore Drive earlier that day. After the fifty-pence piece was returned to his trouser pocket there had followed a row, not a lighthearted exchange of views, but an argument that had left the air thick with blame and discord. It started when Steve had claimed that a "power beyond" had, through the coin, guided their actions. This enraged Martin. It was not often that Steve heard him swear.

"It's a bloody coin, alright?"

" But it landed heads ..."

"What a surprise!"

"But it *did* land heads."

"And it could have landed tails."

"But it didn't," Steve insisted. "We asked it a question and it gave us an answer."

"Look," the older man had tried to reason, "that's enough of that. When you toss a coin it's even money every time. Okay? The way it lands is completely arbitrary, random. Don't go thinking we asked any questions of anybody ... please."

For a moment, like a diver surfacing, Steve had seen sense. Yet almost at once he was submerged once more, seduced by the panorama of a hidden dimension, one in which he now appeared, even to himself, held momentarily a captive.

"And the fact that we chose to make it best of three just goes to show that we were prepared to go on tossing the coin until we got the result we wanted," Martin had tried to finish more generously. "I mean, I've been itching to knock this wall down for weeks. It just helped make it clearer in my mind."

"You're right," Steve conceded.

Yet still Martin had had a point to drive home. "But I don't like it, Steve. We shouldn't have been tossing coins, like idiots. It's not clever. If your mother could have seen us ... and if I hadn't *wanted* to knock this wall down ... I've a good mind to say leave it as it is, just out of spite."

"But that would be bad luck," Steve immediately objected.

"Steve! What have I just said?"

"Sorry."

Martin had been genuinely bad-tempered here. "Just leave it, okay? And listen up: as far as all this gambling goes: I don't want to hear any more of it, all right? That's it. No more bets, no more tips, no more questions, no more tossing coins. And especially no more talk of luck. You'll have plenty of time when you're older to see it's the punters betting the bookies and the bookies getting rich. Do you reckon they've got God on their side, then?"

If it hadn't been for the fact it was still raining when he climbed the steps to street level, a passer could not have been blamed for assuming that Steve was crying.

"You look far away," Mrs Holland whispered; she had evidently been studying him silently.

Steve's thoughts retreated, like so many fish darting to an overhanging riverbank as a shadow advances over their pool. "I was just thinking ..."

"You're in love," said the old lady mischievously. "Don't worry, I'm not telepathic: Mary-Anne told me."

Steve would go along with this: he gave an embarrassed laugh.

"What's her name?"

"Anita."

"What a pretty name! Anita. What does she want to do?"

"She wants to be a dancer and a singer."

"My, how things have changed! In my day a girl's dream was to join The Wrens!"

"I don't think that would appeal to her," Steve said, for a moment his old self.

But as the half-hour played itself out, with the conversation starting and stopping in its staccato fashion, Steve found that sense of isolation return to haunt him. It was not so much the feeling of alienation and distance from those he loved and counted as family that was of concern now, however; it was more the inescapable knowledge that his thinking had found a new energy and direction. It was as if a dam had burst and the weight of water had forged a fresh course through the valley below. Try as he might, he could not alter the path of that flow: it was too late: the sheer volume of draining water was too great. The fear that he was in some way altered, possessed even, was terrifying. Would, or could, he ever be the Steve Marsden of before?

Beyond this there was the question of his relationship with Anita, at once thrown into better definition by the scrutiny of others. Here the mantle of self-deceit was wearing decidedly thin. He could lose himself in her scent when they embraced, his fingers gliding over her skin, so soft it might have been silk – but when they pulled apart ... how much did they really have in common? It would take more than closing a window to exit this game. Steve hung his head in shame. Somehow everything was wrong.

TWELVE

Buzz was in *Accident and Emergency*. It was Mel on Anita's mobile: they must come quick.

Steve and Anita crossed the park in silence. There were groups of students playing football or stood in a circle throwing Frisbees, and they had to skirt these in order not to encroach on their invisible boundaries. Two men playing in a game of five-a-side football wolf-whistled Anita as the couple hurried passed.

"Get lost," she muttered under her breath.

They began the descent into the city centre, and soon had reached the sign that read *Sexual Health*. Fleetingly Steve recalled the afternoon Buzz had stood beneath this sign with Mel looking proudly on. If he had been alone at that moment, he allowed himself to think, hanging back a yard, maybe he and Helena would have gone for a coffee; and maybe once in the café Helena would have broken down, would have been in need of solace and comfort.

They found Buzz and Mel seated just inside the door. The right side of Buzz's face was a mess: red and swollen; above his eye there was a diagonal cut, a deep cut, the parted skin like two new lips. It made your own eyes smart to look at it.

"Bloody hell: what happened Buzz?" Anita whispered.

"His father whacked him, didn't he?" Mel answered.

The sorry story was simply and quickly told. Buzz's father had gone out on the town after work, got pissed up, and had come home looking for a fight. At first Buzz had steered clear of trouble, but his father had got his own way, eliciting from his son the one remark that would excuse his next action (Buzz thought they had quarrelled over the year of the World Cup in Mexico) – and he thumped him. First in the solar plexus, then a jab to the right temple weighted with a full measure of the man's frustration and hatred. Buzz had gone down between two chairs. He had been unconscious for more than five minutes apparently. Meanwhile his father had left the house, slamming the door behind him, as if it were he who had been injured. It was his mother, worse for drink herself, who had brought him round, sloshing cold water over Buzz's neck (as they sat there in *A & E* Steve had noticed that Buzz's collar was soaked with both blood and water). Mel had happened to phone, and was at his house within ten minutes. Together they took a cab to the Infirmary.

Buzz was still shaking. It seemed he couldn't breathe in without shuddering; his chest trembled like the skin on a drum. And try as he might, he could not keep his top lip from moving either. Mel sat to his left with her naked right arm draped over his neck. There was blood on her jaw and chin and collar bone, where she had come into contact with her boyfriend's injury. Anita sat on a chair on the other side. By contrast, she held herself away from Buzz, not wanting to get too close – to the blood or to the misery that Buzz was weathering.

A nurse appeared at the entrance to the row of cubicles. "Ben Fairclough?"

When Buzz rose Steve saw a look of determination stamp itself on his friend's features. He was ready for the stitches that were plainly required; his expression also told of his apparent preparedness for what was doubtless now an uncertain future. The demonstration of raw emotion that he had witnessed, coupled with his friend's acceptance of his pitiable fate, instilled a sense of pride and awe in Steve. What was more, Buzz had Mel, who was still holding his hand as they both moved out of view behind a partition. He relaxed against the back of his chair: his friend would be okay, he knew intuitively.

"They should call Social Services," Anita said.

This remark irritated Steve. It would have been better if Anita had said nothing at all. "What would they do?"

"I dunno. But it's what they're paid for, isn't it?"

About twenty minutes later Buzz and Mel returned to the waiting room. A wad of cotton wool had been plastered over the wound and you could see where the medical staff had swabbed at his bruised and stained flesh. Yet still there was blood streaked on his neck. Buzz looked calmer, though now his top lip was tight with what can only have been pain.

"Eight stitches," Mel announced. "He were a brave lad."

They walked through the automatic doors onto the apron of herringbone block paving, this stained with chewing gum, then stopped, as if they must marshal their thoughts.

"Are you going home, Buzz?" Steve asked.

"He's going to his Nan's," Mel answered for him.

"Where does she live?" Steve queried.

Buzz pointed vaguely west. "In Killbrook: the Mannertson Estate."

"In the Mannertson Estate?" Steve repeated, unable to conceal the surprise in his voice, for this was a notorious area.

"It's only while he gets sorted," Mel explained.

They set off towards the canal. This time it was Mel who dug her hand into Buzz's back pocket. Poor Buzz; he just walked blindly on, arms limply hanging by his side. Presently they passed the diving shop, with the wet-suited man suspended, silent and horizontal, from the ceiling, staring at a seabed of pebbles and starfish. Of all the images collated that afternoon of some weeks before, it was this submerged figure that had somehow impressed itself most forcefully upon Steve's consciousness.

Soon they were at the canal. Above them, half a mile away, some fifteen minutes off, stood the imposing silhouette of the Mannertson Estate. From here the estate resembled a latter-day Stonehenge, with its six towerblocks, honeycombed monoliths, positioned according to some ancient rite. But this utopian model of high-rise living was never out of the local papers. Built in the early Sixties – with external panels of block colour randomly spattered over the concrete render – the architect had seen fit to throw down an intricate maze of paths and narrow alleys which would lead pedestrians in and out of the estate, take them to shops within the stone circle, allow them to visit other tower blocks. The journalists had termed the pathways "slaloms", for it was these conduits of movement, so innocently conceived, that now presented opportunities for ambush and terror. At the circle's core there was a vast arena of garages. Here in the acres of broken and scorched tarmac, the youths congregated to watch their peers demonstrate driving skills in high-performance cars stolen from the city centre. One writer had witnessed such a gathering and, with the young tenants hanging from balconies, lining the pathways, he had likened it to a scene from the movie *Apocalypse Now*. There was also the ubiquitous drug problem that here had burnt deep, like a fire over heather. It was said that you should never wear sandals in the Mannertson Estate: the risk of spiking yourself on a discarded syringe was too great.

The four, like animals in the jungle seeking safety in numbers, seemed to bunch as they passed the first tower block, a silent sentry over the invisible populace behind.

"Where does she live?" Anita whsipered.

"In Concord," Buzz answered. "That one."

They made their way swiftly over the concrete slabs to the entrance of the block, either side of which was positioned two saucer-like planters, once doubtless beautifully pencilled on an architect's plan, now awash with litter and cigarette tabs. Inside, however, the communal area was not so bad. The exterior of the lifts was finished in stainless steel, the walls tiled in a mosaic fashion, lozenges of simple colour, again very Sixties. The lift was waiting at ground level.

Presently they stepped out onto the eighteenth floor. There seemed to be six flats giving off this landing. The door to 212 was ajar; Buzz's Nan may have been watching their ant-like progress at ground level. They filed into the flat, but did not proceed beyond the hallway. Buzz silently embraced his grandmother.

"You'll be okay now," Steve heard her say, as she patted the back of his neck.

The storm of emotion was raging within Buzz once more. "I'm sorry, Nan."

"You're sorry? What have you to be sorry for?"

"I should have kept out of the way."

"Don't let me hear you say that again. Tell your friends to come in."

Mel first, then Steve and Anita pushed through the doorway of the sitting room. Some minutes of introduction followed as Buzz's grandmother carefully scrutinised each of her guests.

"So you're Marsden; I've heard about you," she said to Steve, as he shook her limp hand.

As Mrs Fairclough settled Buzz on the sofa – if anything she was fussing a little too much – Steve found himself drawn to the window, beneath which lay the city, grey, red and black, like a carpet. He could have been a god for the extent of this vista. It was breathtaking. There was the Emley Moor Mast, due south, a needle positioned as if to puncture the sky. Then, closer to home, in the waterfront area, he counted as many as eight cranes. It was not often that you looked down on a crane. They stood like their namesakes, or herons, the latter patiently poised to spear an unsuspecting fish that had come to take the stick-like limb for granted. He would tell Martin of this concentration of building energy, he thought; their next flat should be more central, closer to this hub of activity.

"Do you want juice?" Buzz's Nan offered, pointing at a tray with four glasses and a jug.

They took their drinks. Some minutes of small talk passed,

though no reference was made to Buzz's situation.

Steve returned to the window, as if it were a magnet. For there was a calmness in this Olympian view. While the others murmured around him, Steve bathed in its cleansing action. He had lately been infected by a panic and fear of sorts – now, perhaps on account of the clarity of the panorama before him, he felt momentarily free of the sticky web. Had the Dreamcatcher at last allowed him through? As his eyes moved through the labyrinthine maze of streets below, Lotto's slogan of *It Could Be You* suggested itself to him. If he were a god he would catapult a stone into the void before him, he thought; and the end of its parabolic path would mark the winner. The whole process was as random as Martin had promised: there could be no other way of viewing it when you were looking out at a quarter of a million people, as he was now doing.

"What's your canary called, Mrs Fairclough?" Mel was asking, half stooped to look up into the bird's cage.

"They call him Joey," the old lady replied.

Yet it was not so easy to climb out of the web. You seemed to get some way, then you had to start all over again. For a magic element *must* have been involved in the selection of the four horses of his failed yankee. To get them to come up one after the other was simply beyond the bounds of natural probability. It was like catapulting four stones and the stones landing on the roofs of four blood relations. The odds against it were too great. Steve grimaced. Then to lose faith in the method of the selection in the way he had (or Martin unknowingly had), and so to forfeit it all ... Momentarily he surrendered to the cloying web.

"I said: what happens if there's a fire, Mrs Fairclough?" Anita was asking.

"You've to shut all your doors and sit tight," she answered.

Steve frowned. There was something about Anita's manner that positively irritated him today. She seemed to ask all the right questions, make fitting comments, yet there was a lack of interest or soul in her voice. In the window, superimposed over the mast and the gentle, rolling moors, he observed Mel's reflection. It was no secret that she and Buzz had gone the whole way, and, with this in mind, he studied her from head to toe. She did not have Anita's shoulders and waist, nor her friend's near-perfect features, but she was sexy nonetheless. Very sexy. It was more to do with her manner: she was straightforward, so straightforward you could almost say she was out of reach. If she gave herself to you then that would really mean something.

"But any road, they're designed for fire," Mrs Fairclough finished.

Briefly Steve imagined smoke rising from beneath the doors. That was it. He had had enough. He would leave this place with its vertiginous views. Certainly there was a welcome anonymity to being hidden away here on the eighteenth floor, and there was a warmth in this home with its bird, its simple decorations, its every corner flooded with light – but now he must get out of here, get his feet back on the ground. Furthermore he must be alone. He made his excuses, told each of his friends he would ring them later, and took the lift to ground level.

The first thing you became aware of at ground level was sound: the sound of traffic, of aircraft, of kids shouting in the slaloms. Steve kept his head down. He had learnt from experience that sometimes just one glance, one locking of eyes, was enough to precipitate a confrontation. As he passed the pair of silent sentries – Victory and Temperance – his mobile began to vibrate and ring. He made sure he was clear of their shadow before answering it.

"Steve, it's Vinnie ..."

"Yes, Vinnie."

"I wanna see you."

"Where are you?"

"I'm in the market – packing up."

"I'll be there in ten minutes."

※

As Steve approached the stall he saw Vinnie turn to whisper something to Rich Swift, and then Rich Swift move off immediately.

Vinnie came straight to the point. "That twelve fifty: buried in the sand or spent?"

"What do you mean?"

"I need a grand, I need to borrow a grand."

"What for?"

"Lend me the grand and I'll give you two back by Christmas."

"What do you want it for?" Steve persisted.

"You know I've been in Holland having meetings with the mail order people? Well, I can't do nothing without the Visa swipe machine: can't take any orders, can't do any business. These days you have to front five grand to get the machine: you know, for transactions not honoured. And I'm short of a grand. And I need to start like ... next week."

Steve had been bullied by Vinnie in the past and had shown himself to be a pushover. Thus he had a good mind to reject the request out of hand. But there were some aspects of this that required consideration. First, Vinnie was good for his word, and always had been. There would be little chance of the money vanishing, especially in view of the gold bracelet and the car he had lately acquired, not to mention the bankrolls he had most nights been eager to show his brother. Second, taking his winnings into account, he could well afford to lend his brother a thousand pounds. Third, wasn't this scale of return on his investment exactly what was at present needed (Mrs Holland's money still had not moved from his current account)? And fourth, the thousand would be ring-fenced, so to speak: it could not be lost should Steve get any further into gambling (though who he would find to place the bets after Martin's speech he did not know, what with Buzz's father also being out of the picture).

"When do you want it?"
"Monday."
"Cash or cheque?"
"Either."

THIRTEEN

Martin had not only knocked the two rooms into one, he had also punched through an opening, a hatch, into the kitchen. He was kitchen side, bent down, his head half through the irregularly shaped hole, as if he were about to place his neck on a block. Steve was in the new sitting room, this the size of a squash court.

"Croque monsieur or a croque madam, Mr Marsden?"

"Chips'll do fine."

"A salad of rocket or dandelion leaves?"

"It's amazing, Martin," Steve enthused.

"Not half, eh?"

"I had no idea."

"Well, you know what they say: *He who dares wins.*"

Steve moved to the garden end of the room and stood with his back to the window. It was an overcast morning, yet the space before him seemed to glow with light. Long gone were the days of the empty shelves and crossed off calendar. Martin had been right all along. The proof was in the pudding. For a moment a sense of pride and respect for his stepfather rose in Steve's chest. You could almost cry for the way it made you feel.

Martin was now furthest from him, with his back to the windowsill street-side. In this attitude they could have been about to start their game of squash. Martin seemed to be bending his knees, half-squinting, checking the lines and levels. Steve had seen him do this a few times already; then he would go off, only to return to the checking mode. But this time Martin was frowning slightly. Steve joined him. From here you could see right to the end of the garden.

"Does that look straight to you?" Martin asked, though the question was not really directed at Steve.

"What look straight?"

"The beam," Martin replied, now eager for his stepson's opinion.

"Which beam?"

"Which beam do you think?"

Martin pointed to one end of the beam then to the other, each supported by a column of brickwork perhaps eighteen inches deep, this the only remaining part of the wall which had once divided the floor-space into two rooms. He had a point. If you looked at one end, made a note of its position in relation to the garden window, then looked to the centre of the beam, and compared measurements, it did appear that something wasn't square.

"Must be an optical illusion," Steve volunteered.

Martin would not be placated. "It can't be the beam. It must be the window ..."

But the more you looked at the window, the more level it appeared.

They made their way to the other end of the room. From here, when you went through the same procedure of mentally noting the height of the window in relation to one end of the beam and then comparing it to the point furthest from where it was supported, you could see that something definitely wasn't right. And what was more you could see it wasn't the window that had been installed incorrectly: it was the beam that was sagging. Perhaps by as much as two inches.

"Oh shit," Martin whispered.

Steve turned to face his stepfather. The blood had drained from his top lip.

"What's the matter?" Steve asked in the same whisper.

"Steve, something isn't right."

They made their way to the centre of the room and, heads raised, made a thorough inspection of the brickwork: the brickwork comprising the two pillars, and the brickwork once concealed by the coving. There was evidence of hairline cracks – actually, some proper cracks – in both; but of more concern to the older man was the crazy paving effect of cracking to the newly-plastered ceiling. Martin grimaced like a wolf baring its teeth.

"I think we had better get a jack under there pretty sharpish," he muttered, pointing to a pile of Acro Jacks that he had laid neatly along one wall.

But just then there was a knock, knock, knock on the front door.

"Hellooo, Mr Lenton?"

It was Mr Harris from Flat 1.

"Oh shit," Martin whispered again.

Steve remained out of view as his stepfather paced to the top of the hallway and opened the door.

The lawyer had a singsong voice. "Good morning, Mr Lenton."

"Good morning, Mr Harris."

"Mr Lenton, there's a fissure opened up in my bathroom."

"A fissure?"

"A crack in the wall: I can see daylight through it."

Martin made no reply.

"May I come in?" Mr Harris then asked.

"Well, yes ..."

Both men came to a halt in the doorway of what had been the front sitting room. Mr Harris did not acknowledge Steve, he just stared at the beam, ceiling level. Steve studied the man he sensed was about to play some part in his destiny. Mr Harris was evidently getting ready for work: still in his shirtsleeves, his top button was undone and his tie was draped over one shoulder. He was young, maybe only thirty, yet he had a paunch that had been displaced to hang over a tightly drawn belt.

"That a load-bearing wall?" he asked.

"Yes."

"And you've recently taken it down."

"On Thursday," Martin replied, and there was a note of defeat in his voice, as if he knew they were done for.

"I shall have to check the lease as regards modifications to the fabric of the building."

Martin seemed to rally here. "What do you mean?"

"I don't recall any provision giving leaseholders the facility to make fundamental alterations to the building." Now Mr Harris glanced briefly at Steve, yet still he offered no sign of acknowledgement or greeting. "I mean," he went on, " I own the top-floor flat, but that doesn't give me the right to put on a glass roof."

Martin shuffled awkwardly on his feet.

"Anyway, that's beside the point. We need to get an engineer to inspect this."

"I had an engineer do all the calculations," Martin said, a ring of renewed hope in his words.

Mr Harris withdrew a diary from the back pocket of his trousers. From the spine he produced a thin, silver pen. "May I make a note of his name?"

"Shelldown. Shelldown and Briggs: structural engineers. They're Harrogate based."

"In the meantime I suggest you stop all works forthwith."

"What do you mean?"

"Mr Lenton, this is very serious. We must establish what has gone wrong."

"But ..."

"As I said: a fissure has opened up in my bathroom. You can see into the next room. We must get this looked at," and he waved his silver pen in the air (which, Steve thought, caught the light in the same way as the fifty-pence piece). "Immediately."

There was now a long silence between the three. What was at once plain to Martin and Steve was that Mr Harris had all the time in the world. There was evidently a procedure to be followed in situations of this sort: time was not of the essence.

And once the lawyer had left the flat this impression was to remain, like the odour of his aftershave; it was as if he had cast a spell on the clock. Stepfather and stepson mooched about. Now that they could not work they did not know what to do.

"Come on, we'll have some breakfast" Martin said at last.

As they sat in silence in the café, Steve noticed that today there was no *Daily Mirror*.

In normal circumstances, Martin would play no part in witch-hunts ("Trip on a banana skin and do you know what? It's someone's fault'); but these were, of course, not normal circumstances. His first port of call was Shelldown and Briggs.

They were sitting in the car outside the park gates. (Martin would get some facts before the cat was out of the bag.) The bandstand, for the most part concealed by summer foliage, was just visible. Through a porthole of clearer glass – they had wound up their windows against a drizzle and now the windscreen was opaque with condensation – Steve pictured Anita seated side-saddle on the wooden rail as she had appeared some months before. In his mind's eye, she wore that same mocking expression, at once flirtatious and obdurate. For an instant he heard his heart on his breath. He frowned: it was extraordinary in this moment of crisis and unfolding drama, and extraordinary given his recent feelings towards her, that he should be thinking of her twisted waist and hips, the underside of one thigh yielding to the handrail below.

"254 x 126 x 73 kilos per metre universal beam? That's what you told me to use and that's exactly what I did use ... The what? The material specification? Yes, yes: to the letter. I think it might be a good idea if you came to look at it ... how much? Two hundred and twenty-five pounds? Well, yes ... you'd better. We'll see you this afternoon at three o'clock then."

In the past – in fact just this morning – if Martin had used the term "we", a sense of pride and strength would have risen in Steve's chest. Together, a united team, perfectly complemented, they had beavered away to transform Sycamore Drive for the betterment of the family. Now he wished he had viewed the whole property development idea as Vinnie had done: with a simple, if somewhat amused, detachment.

"Two hundred and twenty-five pounds an hour!" Martin muttered, and for a moment Steve recognised this voice as belonging to the Martin of old, mildly resentful, easily needled by injustices as regards money matters.

The next call was made to Alan Braithwaite, and no sooner had Martin said "Alan Braithwaite, please," than Steve sensed that the blame would come to rest fair and square at this man's door. For it was Alan Braithwaite's small metal working business in the Monkton Hill area that had supplied the beam in the first place. As his stepfather was put on hold, Steve recalled the afternoon they had driven round to Braithwaite's; the bogus, American-style handshake that Alan and Martin had adopted; the girlie calendars; the curtains of acrid smoke that they had had to penetrate to get to Alan's glass-fronted office to one side of the workshop. This was just the kind of place he would *not* do his work experience fortnight in, he remembered himself thinking at the time.

"Alan, I've got a problem ... That beam you supplied me. It was 254 x 126 x 73, wasn't it?"

Pause.

"Yes, the one you delivered to Sycamore Drive."

Another pause.

"All I'm saying is: it was what you said it was, wasn't it?"

Further silence.

"What do you mean, you didn't *inspect* it?"

Martin was pulling at his neck, pinching the loose skin that seemed to glow white and red by turns.

"No, I didn't see any paperwork ... and no, I can't remember a delivery note ..."

Now Martin's hand moved from his neck to his chest.

"Alan, can't you get them to fax a copy through? This is serious. Yes, and I'll come round for it now."

This time as they made their way across the workshop to Alan's office Steve had to raise both hands to his ears. Just inside the concertina doors two men were hammering flush a seam, one throwing the hammer as if it were a whip, the other absorbing the blows with a dollie. Over this there were wails and screams as workpieces surrendered in the chucks of a pair of lathes. Other men were welding, their shadows grotesquely distorted on the walls behind by a light so bright it left a stain on your vision. And there were the clouds of smoke, which hung still, thick and poisonous. This place could have been Hades.

There were no good-humoured pleasantries and no handshakes of any description this time. Alan had a copy of the delivery note and material certificates waiting on his makeshift desk. You could tell there was something wrong just by studying his expression.

"*Ordinarily* we would have inspected it here," Alan explained, his words slow and rounded over the orchestra beyond his office. "The material would have come here and then gone on to you. But my man's been off for over a month now. I told the stockholders to deliver it direct to you: you were in a hurry if you remember."

Martin was grimacing. "So what section was it?"

"What you took delivery of was 254 x 126 x 43 kilos per metre, not 73 kilos per metre as you wanted."

"Or as you ordered?"

"Yes: or as I ordered. Here's my written order, dated June 12th," Alan said, doing his very best to limit the weight of emphasis in his voice, as now he had completely absolved himself of any blame.

"So what's happened?" Martin went on.

"It's that bloody man in Henson's. I'm never going to deal with Henson's again."

"What do you mean, 'that bloody man in Henson's'?"

"I'm afraid they've given you the wrong section."

A siren wailed in the workshop. Immediately the sound of industry ceased. It was as if a conductor had cut the air with one last flourish of his baton. Up to now Steve had watched the exchange between Martin and Alan Braithwaite as he might a movie, a dozen metres back in a darkened auditorium. It could have been *The Titanic*, the cruiser sinking slow and sure, turquoise waters rising within the sealed bulkheads: everywhere Martin turned he was confronted with the same inescapable fact: the way ahead was barred. And now this abrupt silence from the workshop area had brought home the truth in its naked simplicity. Alan Braithwaite must have been aware of this, too, for now his words were softer, quieter.

"This section of beam," he went on, holding up a copy of the delivery note, "has half the strength of this," he finished, waving the written order. "The thickness of the flanges and web is about half. To be quite honest I'm not surprised it's sagged."

Once again Martin crashed ahead in his quest for air. "So it's Henson's fault?"

Now Alan pointed to a disclaimer at the bottom of the delivery note. As he did so he frowned deliberately. "The onus is always on the customer to check the specification, I'm afraid. All the stockholders are the same."

"Bloody hell," Martin muttered, ashen.

"I'm sorry, Martin."

"Not half as sorry as I am."

Still Steve viewed this as if he were watching it on a screen. But now he found he was doing so with more interest – with the interest of a voyeur perhaps. He tried to look away, to absorb himself in the actions of the men beyond Alan's office, who were making their way to a rest area with their lunch boxes – but his eyes kept returning to Martin's reflection in the glass panes. Here was someone in trouble, someone held as if in a trap. It was easy to accept no part in it if you so wished. Then you could indulge in the perverse pleasure of watching the condemned man as he climbed the scaffold, watch him bravely exchange a word with the executioner, watch him as he prepared for the beyond. Once more Steve tried to break his gaze, tried to feel what he should feel. It was to no avail. There just remained with him a strong sense that something was about to happen. What it was he had no idea, of course; but in some strange way that unknown held promise, if only promise of change. And it was all down to Martin.

These were not the thoughts of a kind person, and Steve was relieved when they stepped out onto the street once again.

Now they had established what had gone wrong, there was really no need for the structural engineer to endorse their findings. Yet Martin did not cancel the appointment. Mr Shelldown appeared in the basement area on the stroke of three. He was wearing a yellow hard hat and a pair of safety spectacles. He spent some minutes pacing up and down the open-plan room, paying particular attention to the new doorframes that Martin had fitted. All the mitred joints had sprung open.

"It's very serious," he pronounced finally.

FOURTEEN

Needless to say, there was, on this occasion, a quite different atmosphere in the sitting room of Stanningley Terrace as they took their places at the round table.

Before them lay a letter that Mr Harris had written from his office later that morning, then seen fit to have sent by motorbike courier (he must have known their address from when he sold on the survey). In fact, Mary-Anne had read this letter several hours before Martin and Steve had pushed through the front door, heads down, at 4.30. Thus she was perhaps more fully acquainted with their predicament than they were. She had not summoned them home on the mobile: maybe she had needed time to digest the information in private, just as Martin had needed time to gain a better perspective of their situation. There had been no apparent intonation of blame or sadness in her voice, just an "Oh, Martin ..."

Mr Harris's letter was upside down, yet Steve could decipher excerpts of the bold type: **"Further to our meeting of this morning I must insist that all works cease forthwith pending engineer's reports"**; and **"hold you responsible for all costs associated with reinstatement"**; and **"in the absence of insurances"**; and **"prudent to set up an account from which expenses can be met in respect of ..."**

"Right," Mary-Anne began, placing her hands before her on the polished wood. "I just want to say first of all that I have no doubt that we can all come through this ... but we must do it together. And we must take it slowly, one step at a time ..."

"Mary-Anne," Martin tried to cut in, as if now he must make

some form of official apology, "I'm so terribly, terribly ..."

Mary-Anne waved him down. "Let's focus on what's before us."

Steve was still staring at the lawyer's letter; he would not meet Martin's eyes. He may have viewed the calamity with a measure of detachment at Braithwaite's, but now it was time to apportion blame, to have that pound of flesh, it seemed. They had taken their places at the table, but in reality Steve was not sitting equidistant between his mother and stepfather, as he had done at their previous meetings: he had unconsciously come to sit closer to his mother. In this attitude Martin appeared to be under interrogation: it was two against one.

"As always we must consider in the first instance what's coming in," Mary Anne deliberately continued. "As you know, my work has pretty much dried up. This is a bad season, granted – it's always been slow in the summer – but these last two years have been different. I'm just not getting the volume of work I used to. And Martin hasn't been bringing home any money ... I know, I know ..."

Here she must wave down Martin a second time.

For a moment Steve was transported back to that night some months before when Martin had summarised his plans for the renovation of Sycamore Drive. How foolish they had been to allow themselves to be seduced by his spreadsheet of figures, contrived to show a profit in bold at the foot of the page! In hindsight it was so glaringly obvious that these plans would come to naught. Indeed it was as if those columns of figures were serpents, just biding their time before rising to lodge a deadly venom. A wave of anger broke over Steve. Why didn't he just stand up and punch his stepfather?

"So ... I've made some notes here ... Our income these last two months has been, well, four hundred and eighty-five pounds. That's what I've earned. Against this we have all the usual household expenses, including energy bills, which I calculate to be in the region of eight hundred pounds per month."

Steve was jolted out of his reverie. Seen in this context alone it seemed incredible that they had allowed themselves the privilege of any involvement in the property market at all. Then he sank back into his reflections. Talk about plans coming to naught, Martin's further plans. How after Sycamore Drive there would be two properties, then four. How, subsequent to this, there would be holidays away, to places like Miami, New York, Las Vegas! Las Vegas! Steve's focus deepened. The force of his first blow had put Martin on the floor, and now he was tearing at his stepfather's face, gouging, spitting, scratching.

"Beyond that there are the mortgage payments on Sycamore Drive ... We've borrowed seventy-two thousand pounds to date and the bank's charging us six and a half percent. I calculate that at three hundred and ninety pounds per month."

They should get rid of Martin, he then considered. It would be like prising a limpet off a rock, but they must get rid. Desperate measures were in order. He, Steve, would go on hunger strike: refuse to eat until his stepfather had left for good. He pictured himself, his face bleached of colour, waving away food, waving away doctors. His mother needed protecting: who else would deal with Martin if it were not for him? Mary-Anne had paused before drawing a deeper breath.

"In addition we will have the engineer's and surveyor's fees for their reports; then ultimately the costs of repairing the building should it come to that. I've no doubt there will be other expenses that I haven't thought of yet. For instance, there'll probably be compensation to pay the other flat owners whilst the work is in progress, that or they'll move out temporarily and we'll have to pay for their accommodation, that kind of thing ... So, as far as I can see it, we don't have many options. At the end of the day, admittedly, we're going to have the flat in Sycamore Drive, but in the meantime what *are* our options? So far as I can see it we must either rent out this house ... or sell it."

"Mary-Anne!" Martin interjected.

Mary-Anne looked bad-tempered for the first time. "Well, have you got any better ideas?"

"Yes, I'll go back out to work for one."

"Dear Martin, even if you worked all the hours God gives it wouldn't make any impression on this."

This flash of impatience arrested Steve's thoughts. He glanced at his mother afresh. Mary-Anne may have fussed about trivial matters, but any real difficulties and setbacks were met by a stubborn pragmatism, a sort of bedrock of common sense. Was this the same strength she had drawn upon to cope with his father's sudden death, he briefly wondered?

"But we mustn't be rushed into anything," the other protested. "Lawyers make their living by frightening people – you know that as well as I do."

"We mustn't be rushed: you're absolutely right. But at the same time we must do something: it wouldn't be right to do nothing. And having established that we must do something, then we should do it ... and sooner rather than later."

Martin conceded this point with a weighted nod of the head.

"So I propose we let this house. We probably should be grasping the nettle ... but I don't think I could bear just selling up next week."

Here was the first resonance of bitterness in Mary-Anne's voice. There was also a tear glistening in the corner of one eye.

"But at least we will have something coming in," she finished, stronger.

"And where will we live?" Steve asked. "Where will we live?"

"Well, of course, that is something we'll have to research."

There was a silence. Steve heard himself swallowing, nothing more. It was as if he were standing before a black hole, his feet perilously close to the edge.

"I spoke with Mr Williams from the agency this afternoon," Mary-Anne went on quietly. "It would appear we could get as much as one thousand, two hundred and fifty pounds per calendar month for this house."

Another pause.

"So I've told them to put it on their books with immediate effect."

To hear the words "immediate effect" was jarring: it was enough to catapult you into that abyss, your arms stretched before you (like the figures on the tarot card) to break your fall in the pit of that coal-black hole.

"What: you mean tomorrow?" Martin asked, barely daring to meet Mary-Anne's eyes.

"Yes, I mean tomorrow," she answered quietly.

ॐ

"Prize dipstick!"

"Vinnie ..."

"What a plonker!"

The pendulum had swung the other way: there now existed a well of sympathy, perhaps nourished by guilt, for Martin. "It wasn't his fault."

"Whose fault was it then?"

"The steel stockholder's fault."

Vinnie was typing a text message into his phone as he spoke. "Steel stockholder's fault!" the older brother scoffed. "It's Martian Martin, isn't it? What an idiot."

"And Mum's going to let the house."

"She told me."

"You going to stay with us?"

"I'll stop with Rich."

"You don't sound very bothered ... as if you care."

Vinnie shrugged, palms rotated skywards. "What can *I* do? I don't like the idea of you guys living in bed and breakfast accommodation, but really: what can I actually do about it?"

Steve could not reply to this at first. His thoughts seemed to scatter, like a cloud of sparrows exploding into the air. "Who said anything about bed and breakfast accommodation?" he stammered at last.

"So where are you going to live then?"

"Well, I don't know," he honestly replied.

Vinnie was typing another message into his mobile: his lack of feeling needled Steve.

"I'd like that thousand back," he then said.

Now Vinnie stopped typing. "You what?"

"I'd like that money back."

"I told you: I need it."

"Well, *I* need it now."

"You lent it to me: I can't get it back."

"What do you mean you can't get it back?"

"I've had to lay it out."

This expression and explanation needled Steve further. "You said you wanted it for the swipe machine."

"That's right. The five thousand has to sit in an account. For contingencies."

Another irritating expression.

"Well, I want it back."

Vinnie was firm now. "Steve, you lent it to me in good faith. I can't give it you back yet. Okay? And anyway there's no sense in throwing good money after bad."

"What do you mean?"

"If they're going to go bankrupt, then they're going to go bankrupt. What's the point in you losing money as well?"

"I can't believe you just said that, Vinnie."

"Well, I did say it. I'm just being realistic. Sometimes in life you have to separate your feelings from the stuff you have to deal with."

Steve walked off without commenting. He was soon lost in the crowds of the indoor market.

୶

The old cemetery, choked by undergrowth, self-seeded trees rising between plots, resembled the ruins of an ancient civilisation. A great many of the headstones were crooked, out of plumb, having subsided into the yielding earth. Others had been pushed over, perhaps by vandals, perhaps even by council workers whose brief it was to render the weighted Victorian stonework safe – to both visitors and marauding youths alike. Steve could not help it: but the scene of devastation recalled the basement flat in Sycamore Drive.

The motorway was very apparent from here. You could not actually glimpse the broad ribbon of tarmac on account of the tall foliage, each branch and sapling twisting towards the life-giving sun; but owing perhaps to its being concealed, the traffic was more audible than it might otherwise have been. It was weird to walk through this tunnel of leaves, the dead beneath your feet, the living moving all around you, their passage resonating through the air like a thousand aircraft.

Steve paused by a row of common graves. One headstone commemorated the remains of twelve men, women and children buried in January 1901. It was incredible but the oldest person in that plot had only lived to the age of fifty two. And of the twelve, there were three children under six and two babies. It made you feel fortunate even to have reached the age of sixteen. Every four or five rows, randomly placed, stood headstones of the War Graves Commission. These were white and low and invariably in perfect condition. It was difficult to read the lettering against the white sandstone, and even harder to make out the regimental motifs. Sometimes there were two headstones positioned side by side. Friends? Pilot and co-pilot? Officer and batman? Seeing that limited action had taken place in this country, were there really mortal remains in these plots, he wondered – or were the headstones simply memorials at which relatives could pay their respects?

As you stepped out of the old cemetery and into the new it was of course the motorway that drew your eyes, like a magnet. If you looked hard enough, you could fancy that you were able to distinguish drivers and passengers seated upright in their vehicles; in reality you could not, as the six lanes were over a quarter of a mile away. Where were all these people going, it was hard not to ask of yourself in a place like this? What was the rush?

Bottom right, below a gate and drive of gravel, a team from the council was finishing a grave. Rather they were packing up for the night, reversing a small digger onto a trailer, folding up the square of Astro Turf which had served to conceal fresh soil from the mourners just departed. Steve knew exactly where he was going and chose a route that would take him furthest from this cluster of men.

The last time he had come to his father's grave it had been on New Year's Day 1997. He had been eight. He could not remember much about it, save his mother saying after lunch (had they all had lunch in *The George* in town – Mary-Anne, Martin, Vinnie, Mrs Holland and himself?) that she wanted "to see Edmund". Only Steve and Mary-Anne had gone, for some reason. They had stood in silence before the headstone of granite, a canopy of leafless branches ahead of them shrouding the old cemetery like a haze. Mary-Anne had brought a lily – she must have known that she would visit the cemetery after all – and the waxy white petals and the short cropped grass, to all intents and purposes dead for the duration of the winter, made incongruous bedfellows. Steve had shed a tear; Mary-Anne, with pursed lips, had just stared blindly at the chiselled inscription: Edmund Henry Marsden, 1952-1992, RIP.

Now Steve stopped before that same headstone. At his back he could hear the wagon starting up, then moving off, most probably to the depot. All the while the motorway sounded in his ear, like the crashing of surf in a seashell. It was impossible to predict how you would feel, visiting a loved one in this manner. It was not until you were standing there, as if at the bottom of a bed, that you knew whether you would break down, or whether you would be struggling to feel anything whatsoever. This evening Steve felt nothing: he could not see his father, could not feel him, could not sense him. All there was was a rectangle of slightly greener grass, this just sunken from the original where the soil had settled over the past thirteen years. And nothing more.

Steve tried to speak to his father: "Dad, I'm sorry," he apologised – for what he had no idea – but his words were lost in the incessant drone of traffic. "Dad, can you hear me?" he asked, knowing full well that his question would remain unanswered and yet determined to ask it all the same. He frowned. There was no solace or comfort to be found in this place. Not today at any rate. The realisation made him feel utterly alone. But now he sensed why he had come to the cemetery for the first time in eight years.

Viewed in the cold light of day it seemed that they might well lose Stanningley Terrace. Certainly they could reverse their immediate fortunes by getting some rent in, as his mother called it. But should the engineer's reports on Sycamore Drive turn out bad, as they already tacitly anticipated, then the house would have to go – and with it this link to the past. Steve had really come to say goodbye. Now his eyes filled with tears of sadness. But what was the point of the past if it was so unresponsive? he asked of himself; and there was a real edge of impatience and pique in his thoughts. Why didn't his father offer him a sign, some form of encouragement?

Steve turned and walked the length of the row of graves, as if he were a general inspecting his troops. Many of them had black headstones with a scene, an image, chiselled chalk-white to one side of the lettering. On one there was a winding road leading up to a mountaintop village, the head of the road concealed by a sudden turn behind a tower; another had a saxophonist bending beneath the weight of his instrument, his right heel raised in a manner of keeping time; there was even one view of a candle before a casement window, a silent moon beyond. A great number of the stones shared a common inscription: *Good Night, God Bless*; or *Gave So Much, Took So Little*.

Steve returned to his father's grave for the last time. He was determined to feel something, even if it was only to feel sorry for himself or to weather a sense of shame that he had come to this place just in a moment of emergency. But as he stood there, almost forcing the tears, something beneath the headstone – something white – caught his attention. Why he had not seen it before he could not imagine – but there, in a small glass jar, someone had placed a flower, a white carnation. He stepped forward to take a closer look. The petals were perfectly fresh, the water in the jar – a honey jar or something similar – was absolutely clear. Bending over it you could almost smell the sweet perfume of the bloom. An expression of intense curiosity displaced his former look of ambivalence. Now he scanned the row of headstones: had someone placed a flower beneath any of these as well? No, they had not. Had his mother been to the cemetery before him? It was the only explanation, yet he did not sense it to be the correct one. He stepped forward to study the jar once more. It was not a honey jar but the type in which you buy baby food, a type not seen in Stanningley Terrace for fifteen years. Steve's frown deepened.

FIFTEEN

"Just yesterday David won £17,650 on Slots ... Gary won £10,950 on Blackjack ... Leyton won £9,500 on Blackjack ... Khasnat won £8,073 on European Roulette ... Who knows, in just a few minutes you could be the one celebrating the biggest win of your life, all courtesy of casinocasino.'

It was strange: these people had won quite large sums on their various games, but in casinocasino's "Practice Mode" Steve had to date won quite a lot more – sixty-three thousand, five hundred and sixteen pounds, to be exact.

Whenever you shut the computer down, the account froze and the balance was carried over to your next session. Thus he had won this amount over a period of weeks, not at one sitting. Admittedly casinocasino started you off with five thousand, but Steve had not once fallen below this figure.

Certainly money could be lost. You could just sit there putting a thousand pounds over and over on red or black. And you would lose, as sure as eggs is eggs. You could also randomly scatter the counters over the green baize (what Steve erroneously called a spread bet) and in that case you would lose, too. But if you took your time, really concentrated, really let the numbers suggest themselves to you – then you could be a winner.

As he sat before the monitor, a milky light bathing his face and neck (the curtains were partially drawn), Steve surrendered to a feeling of exhaustion that seemed to wash against his body as if it were an ocean. The events of the past forty-eight hours were almost too much to comprehend and assimilate: he could not view what had happened, or what awaited them, with any sense of perspective. It was like trying to see both near and far at the same time: one part of the image invariably stayed out of focus. Beyond that, the images were now accompanied by very real physical sensations: over and over he must weather Martin's horror at his simple mistake; taste the sadness and disappointment which his mother had done her utmost to conceal. In addition he had come to feel a needle-like guilt at his complicity in their downfall. Of course the decision to fit the beam had been Martin's, but if he had not precipitated it in the manner he had ... Or had there really been a purpose behind Steve's involvement? Guilt had a habit of making you justify your actions, distorting the truth to absolve yourself of blame. All these images and thoughts distracted him from grasping the situation. It seemed that the playing of this game of chance was the only form of solace and balm available to him: the rhythmic tumbling of the ball did assist you in ordering and tempering your reflections.

Steve's preferred bets involved placing the counters between numbers, either between two numbers (the splits) or four (a corner bet). If you won on these you were paid seventeen-to-one and eight-to-one respectively. He dragged a £500 counter on to the intersection of 10, 11, 13 and 14.

Tick, tick, tick, tick went the ball over the wheel. If you blinked repeatedly, to produce a sort of stroboscope effect, your eyes could distinguish the number quicker than if you tried to follow the slowing revolutions.

"Black 11 ... Player's a winner," the voice announced. And then top right on the screen: You have won £4,000.00 GBP.

It would be some days (or weeks even), of course, before they received the engineer's report. In the meantime there was just the knowledge, already heavily underscored by the individuals concerned, that these professionals were well practised in taking their time. If you were the underdog, the last thing you could expect was for them to march to your tune. Martin had been depressed and elated by turns. One moment he tried to persuade you that all the houses in Sycamore Drive had settled over the hundred years in which they had faced the elements – it was "par for the course". The next he was crestfallen: they were ruined: it was Harris who was the problem: he was going to throw the book at them. Steve had been back to the flat once since that fateful morning. Now a line of Acro Jacks stood beneath the beam like a beaded curtain. Otherwise the empty rooms, hollow and dry smelling, were as they had left them – save that Martin had repeatedly washed the floors clean, as if by scrubbing the shuttered concrete he could in some way eradicate or, at any rate, lessen the impact of his error.

"How bad is it really, Martin?" Steve had asked.

Martin had returned the other's expression of naivety with a look of complete dejection. "Well, I suppose it can't be any worse than the rebuild figure – and that's a hundred and thirty-eight thousand."

"The rebuild figure?"

"That's the amount it's insured for. If the whole bloody place burnt to the ground," he spat, "that's what it would cost to rebuild it."

Steve dragged four £500 counters on to the baize. He was concentrating now on the bottom end of the table, from 18 onwards.

Tick, tick, tick.

"Zero ..."

He laughed to himself: sometimes it was more interesting to lose than to win.

When Steve had shown Martin this roulette game on his computer some two weeks before, he had done so with a sense of trepidation. Would his stepfather be shocked, horrified? Would he report this clandestine activity to Mary-Anne? (Steve was of course quick to explain that this was "Practice Mode" only and, being a minor, he was not eligible to register for *Play For Real* even if he wanted to.) But Martin's initial comment had been only: "European roulette

– that's something then."

"What do you mean?" Steve had asked.

"In America they play with two zeros. The house has double the margin."

"What do you mean?"

"You hit a single number and the bank pays thirty-five-to-one. There're thirty-six numbers, right? And normally one zero. That makes thirty-seven. If there are two zeros ..."

"Is that how the casinos win? With a margin of two or three?"

"That's precisely how they win."

To Steve this seemed incredible, since no account was taken here of luck.

He dragged six £500 chips onto the chequered table. This time he made no effort to summon the winning number from within; indeed he made a point of closing his eyes as he scattered the £3,000. How would Lady Luck see that?

Tick, tick, tick.

And where would they live? he now asked of himself, hardly bothering with the ball as it danced into its slot. Mary-Anne had been silent on this subject. There had been some phone calls made from the privacy of her bedroom, but as yet no family meeting or discussion on the matter. Was she thinking of renting from the same agent who had already shown one couple around Stanningley Terrace and who had another couple booked in for later that morning?

"Black 17 ... Player's a winner," the voice announced. You have won £2,500.00 GBP.

After Martin's explanation of the house's margin, there had followed a debate about whether they were gaming "on a level playing field".

"It's got to be rigged," Steve had insisted.

Once again Martin surprised him. "They don't need to cheat," he murmured as they navigated through the site.

"You sure?"

"Look in FAQs. That'll be the first thing they tell you about, bet you."

Martin was right. *Frequently Asked Questions* was headed *Game Fairness*, and addressed the questions casinocasino had anticipated of its sceptical audience. For instance: *How Do you Prove Your Random Number Generator Is Unbiased? Can The Casino Benefit From A Biased Random Number Generator? What Is The Seed?* The answer to this last question enthralled Martin. He read it aloud twice.

"The seed of a random number generator is the initial point from which a sequence of randomly generated numbers starts. To ensure that a sequence of numbers will not repeat itself if we restart the gaming server, the seed is calculated using as many external factors as possible (e.g. the time of day, system settings, network activity, and many more)."

"That, my friend, is chance personified," Martin had triumphantly said.

Happy days indeed!

Buzz was high: you could see it in his eyes and in his smile.

"Buzz, you're stoned ..."

"So?"

"What have you taken?"

"Just draw."

"Come on."

"A bit of whizz then."

"Whizz?"

"Amphetamine sulphate: speed."

"What do you want to take that for?"

"Because I want to get out of it," Buzz answered honestly.

"That's not good, Buzz." But there was a lack of conviction in

Steve's words. "That's not good, you know," he tried to repeat.

"It's nowt different to going on holiday," Buzz then said. "Only it's cheaper 'cos you get to stay at home. And do you know what? I feel I'm due a bloody holiday."

Steve would not reply to this. He tried to stare his friend out; but Buzz was gazing out of the window, his expression alight with its artificial glow. It seemed Buzz could hold the same posture without moving a muscle for minutes at a time. Perhaps he, Steve, should try some of this drug; he needed a holiday as much as anyone, didn't he? The prospect held no promise, however: there was no quickening of the pulse, no murmur of curiosity to gratify. The sound of a ticking clock filled the air. And then the closing of a door. It was Mel. She may have worn the same vacuous expression: Steve couldn't properly tell.

"You're out of it as well ..."

"Am I chuff."

Unlike Buzz, Mel held Steve's eyes. Indeed she looked down on him from her position at the doorway in an almost dismissive manner, as if this were some form of contest. She wore just a T-shirt, maybe one of Buzz's, which was as short as a mini skirt. Her legs were marble-white. It was Steve who had to look away first. He was suddenly alarmed. If Mel was lying to him, that made the situation a whole lot worse.

"Sorry to hear about the stuff you're going through," Buzz murmured.

"Who told you?" Steve demanded, a defensive ring in his words.

"Anita did. So where are you going to live, then?"

"Who said anything about living anywhere?"

"Anita said you were letting your house ... to get some brass in. So where are you going to live?

"I dunno."

"My Nan's gone to Bridlington for a fortnight: you can stop here," Buzz offered, and he waved a wan hand over the view below, as if he were a king waving from the colonnade of his castle at the kingdom before him, which unfolded, black and red, to the horizon.

A dense silence settled over the three. The sound of the clock was louder this time. Fleetingly Steve saw himself pulling a suitcase through the door, a guest in Concord Tower. Initially a sense of excitement filtered through his veins: here you could be lost, immune from the forces at play at ground level – you would know they were there, but they wouldn't know where to find you. Then this excitement was displaced by the type of fear that makes you want to hold onto the seat of your chair: at any moment you might be tossed to ground level, as if you were a bone thrown nonchalantly down to waiting dogs by an ogre. He could not live in this place. Please God that it would not come to that!

"I'm okay," Steve finally said.

"Suit yourself," Buzz nodded, his words once again devoid of feeling.

"What are you doing for money?" Steve asked.

Now Buzz looked more interested. "I'm going to sell some of them *Big Issues*."

"You're not ..."

"Bloody am!"

"How you going to manage that then? You need to be homeless."

"My cousin's boyfriend has been registered for years. I'll use his card: he's in Spain selling them time-shares."

"But you're a minor."

"They won't know that." (And Buzz was right about this: he had always appeared older than his years). "And you can make good money if you put in the hours," he drawled. "If you start early enough you can make decent money."

"Won't you shurrup about your money?" Mel hissed, and for an instant these words brought an image of the four of them at Whitby to Steve's mind's eye, with gulls hanging in the air and surf thundering against the granite pier.

Buzz shrugged. "What's a life without money? Without things?" he said. And here he sounded just like his father. "A bloody waste of time, that's what it is!"

"I'm just sick of hearing about it: that's all," Mel spat. "It's money this, money that."

Now Steve was convinced that Mel was high too. She shared her boyfriend's countenance, by turns serene and irascible, an unlikely combination. The sight of the two of them, so far away, beyond reach, in fact, filled him with panic. He needed to be in the company of family, of those who loved and knew him.

ॐ

"You'll be fine, you'll be grand," Mrs Holland was saying.

"But we'll probably have to sell the house."

"It won't come to that, I'm sure."

There was a plaintive, self-pitying ring to Steve's words. "It's the lawyer, Mr Harris: Martin says he's going to ruin us."

"Not even Mr Harris is above the law," Mrs Holland replied reassuringly. "You'll see."

"We don't know where we're going to be living ..."

Mrs Holland waved him down. "Steve, Steve," she whispered, "don't think I haven't every sympathy for what you're all going through. Leaving Stanningley Terrace is going to be an upheaval, there's no question about that. But it won't be forever: trust me. And in the meantime you must remember that it's what goes on in here," she patted her left collarbone, "it's how you feel inside that's the important thing ... the most important thing of all."

Now she gestured over the lawn, where once again a gathering of residents had formed a circle with their tables and chairs.

"I know it's hardly the same: but when a new person arrives at Greenglades, they either cope with the change or they don't. Those who do have a sort of inner strength, a strength that enables them to be happy in whatever situation they find themselves. They are not necessarily religious – of course, that can help in some cases – but they seem to have a sort of ... I don't know how to explain it ... a knowledge that whatever obstacles are thrown in their paths they will manage ... more than that, in fact, they will be perfectly content. It's where you are in here that matters, not where you are outside," she finished.

Steve was staring at the squares of carpet beneath his feet. The old lady's words were all very well but, he was considering, when they moved out of Stanningley Terrace, how could they function as a family? Where would the computer be situated? And what about access to the Internet? Where would he watch television after school? Would he be able to sit alone in the evenings, away from Mary-Anne and his stepfather, if he felt that way inclined? He had a right to have these questions answered, he thought with real force, yet so far no one had addressed them. Would he be able to have Anita round? Or Helena? The incongruity of this last reflection caused him to wince.

"Does that make sense?" Mrs Holland asked.

"I went to see Dad," Steve blurted.

Mrs Holland did not answer at first. She fixed him with her watery grey eyes. There was almost a look of caution in her expression.

"I half imagined you had," she answered.

"Someone had put a flower by the headstone."

"A flower?"

"Yes, in a glass jar."

Mrs Holland did not volunteer any comment.

"It wasn't you?" Steve questioned.

"I'm hardly going to take the bus up Beckwith Hill," Mrs Holland laughed, this with the raised eyebrows of "how could you be so silly?'

"I know. I know," Steve backtracked. "Do you think it was Mum?" he then asked.

Mrs Holland's expression was more serious now. "Have you asked her?" she enquired.

"I didn't want to," Steve replied.

"Why not?"

"We never discuss the past."

"What's the present without the past?" Mrs Holland murmured cryptically and, closing her eyes, sank into one of her silences.

SIXTEEN

The right-hand side of Raff's cardigan, the side with the telephone in the pocket, was so weighed down it was virtually at knee level.

"And have you any plans for moving? Not now: I mean in the future. Yes. Yes. Because I can see a house on a hill, not necessarily in the country, but there's a view I can see from one of the windows; you can see quite far. There's something telling me that you will be moving ... and sooner rather than later. Okay?"

Raff was in more of a hurry today. She was preparing a sauce, a tomato or meat sauce. One by one she took down the small jars of herbs and spices from a rack over the cooker; and one by one she placed them on the work surface after she had used them: she was in too much of a rush to screw the tops back on and return them to their former position on the shelf. This would be Anita's job: Steve had seen this procedure adopted before.

"And now I'm seeing aeroplanes. Are you thinking of travelling? Not moving abroad; but travelling, on holiday, for instance. Yes, well I'm getting a good feeling about that. If you get the chance you should definitely go. Just take the plunge because if you don't ... well, time can pass us by, can't it? Okay?"

Anita was painting her nails. With her head bent in an attitude of concentration and her hair bunched in one ponytail, the ladder of vertebrae at the back of her neck was revealed in perfect definition. The flesh about her throat seemed to glow with health and vitality. Steve studied her expression of solitary focus. Lately she had plucked her eyebrows to the point where only a thin line of hair remained. It had made her look fiercer, less willing to compromise on any issue not to her liking. She wore a T-shirt of dark blue with the initials *DG* stamped over her breasts, only it was not a designer name that was written underneath, rather it was *Dead Gorgeous*.

"Is there a John or a James on the other side? A James then? Well, James is saying that you've to go with your intuition. He's saying *'Just do it because you won't regret it'*. Does that make sense? Okay, love: goodbye."

Raff took the handset from her cardigan pocket and replaced the receiver. "Anita, a tin of tomatoes please," she said impatiently, indicating the cupboard to her right. Then the phone began to ring again. "Bloody hell," she muttered. "Bloody *hell*."

There followed a few seconds of exaggerated activity as, the phone ringing all the while, Raff carefully squeezed the telephone back into her pocket. Finally the ringing stopped.

"Is that Edward? *Hello*, Edward. Is there anything specific you wanted to ask me about this afternoon?"

A long pause.

"No," Raff said with a finality that Steve had not heard before, "your accident *was* an accident. I've got a very strong feeling about that. It was not fate: it just happened, okay? Don't think of it as anything other than an accident – you mustn't. It's dreadful, unfortunate, and the timing is bad, but these things happen, don't they?"

Steve was thinking of Helena, his thoughts in the open, swimming like fish about the legs of a predator, since long gone were the days of worry and anxiety where the transparency of thought was concerned. (Indeed, he was now in the habit of thinking, if Raff could read his mind, then she was welcome to it; it might even assist in precipitating the conclusion of his relationship with Anita.) He was asking of himself: if it had been Helena rather than Anita that he had been with, would the past few weeks have unfolded in the manner that they had? Because if he, Steve, had been some form of a catalyst in the chain of events that had led to their undoing, then wouldn't Helena have had some bearing on him and therefore on their situation – and wouldn't it have been a benevolent bearing? Would they be in the desperate situation in which they now found themselves?

"Go into the country with your partner or a good friend," Raff was saying. "Sit under a tree and just let yourself relax. All the time, think of a loved one on the other side, someone who meant a great deal to you and who you miss. Take six portraits of your friend ... and when you have the pictures developed you might be surprised. You might see a sign there – it works for me."

What was all this rubbish? Steve could hear himself silently demanding. He had not of course been invited into Helena's house, yet he was sure it was nothing like this one, with its vault-like walls of subterranean brick. His eyes distanced as he considered Helena's father. Would he soon be dead, lying like his own father in a cemetery amongst a thousand others, the drone of a motorway fixed in his deaf ears? Steve shuddered. Why were his thoughts so morbid? Was it because Raff was always referring to the "other side" – that place from which spirits spoke only to her and to no one else?

Anita looked up, placed the bottle of nail-varnish on the table before her and stood. She gestured to Steve, and they made their way out of the room and up the stairs. There was something aloof in Anita's manner as she closed the door to her bedroom and moved to the full-length mirror by the side of her chest of drawers. Steve came to stand behind her and wrapped his arms around her midriff.

"Careful of my nails," she murmured.

Steve breathed the scent of Anita's hair and her neck. He tried to nibble her earlobe, but she shrugged her shoulder to push his chin away. Now he tried to bury his nose in the scallop of warm flesh above her collarbone, but again she resisted. In light of his reflections of only ten minutes before, Steve was a hypocrite, and a spineless one at that. And he knew it. But he needed Anita – he needed to lose himself in her smell, in her essence, so vague, so ineffable, so difficult to grasp. He tried to lead her to the bed. Once more she resisted; but this time she turned to face him. One of her pencil-thin eyebrows was raised higher than the other.

"Steve?"

"Yes."

"I wanted to talk to you ..."

Steve felt his blood run a little colder, sensing there was something of significance to follow.

"I think we should cool it a bit," Anita said, not meeting his eyes.

"What do you mean?"

"I think I need a little space. A bit of time apart."

ಧ

As Steve crossed town he realised that there were two ways of reacting to Anita's declaration. He could either nurse a broken heart – forever taste her lips, breathe her perfume, feel her fingers over his shoulders – or else he could stand back, as if on dry land, and with that firm ground beneath his feet, view the situation with a degree of equanimity. But there was a knife-edge between the two and he must do everything in his conscious power to channel his thoughts towards the least painful path. The sight of McDonalds, for instance, where he had often met up with Anita, was enough to bring tears to his eyes. So, too, the entrance of The Odeon, in whose flickering auditorium they had kissed and cuddled, losing themselves in one another. In such places he must keep placing obstacles, as if he were damming a river, pushing the bubbling water into an eddy where it had no business to be.

It being a Friday evening made this running of the gauntlet no less difficult, since the centre of town was filling with groups of young people getting ready for an evening out. Head down, eyes trained on the pavement, Steve took the most direct route home. Just north of the station, where the cranes were concentrated, he entered the banking and service industry area. But there were bars and restaurants here, too – some of which had opened in the six-month period since he had last walked through these streets of tall, imposing buildings. Tables and chairs of bright aluminium spilt out onto the pavements, like a lava flow – here sat young men in their shirtsleeves, their attaché cases pinched between their legs, and their female counterparts, likewise dressed in the white and black of the sector's dress code.

Perhaps the deeds to Stanningley Terrace were in a safe in one of these buildings, Steve thought; and he carefully inspected each bank and building society he passed, from its glazed façade at street level, to the top floor windows, dark behind heavy eaves. A wave of frustration broke over him, as if those deeds belonged to him. Of course he understood that they had had to relinquish control over Stanningley Terrace in order to borrow money, but never before had he felt so impotent. The banks would carefully take what was theirs, exacting fees and tariffs that would filter down to do no more than pay for the drinks which he could see were being ordered with a wave of a hand. It was these people who would dictate their future now. Behind their desks, wearing the mantle of their profession, they would decide with the flourish of a pencil, whether Steve and his family would have a home or not. It made you want to throw a brick through one of those windows, to watch the splintering glass cascade to the pavement.

Steve turned left, away from Queen's Court. Ahead there was the usual concentration of cars outside San Petino, momentarily at a standstill as passengers alighted. And once again there was the *Big Issue* vendor in his anorak of blue, bidding drivers forward with one hand, waving gaily with the other. As Steve approached he fancied he could actually see the man's gums as he grinned his toothless grin, and smell his clothing, damp and sweet. Would this be Buzz in a few months? he wondered. Come to that, would this be him, Steve Marsden, in a few months? So engrossed was he in this shocking thought that, just adjacent to the restaurant's entrance, flanked by the planters of eucalyptus and gravel, he found he must sidestep two women who were making a beeline for the glass doors. Their scent filled his nostrils and a flash of gold all but blinded him as the last of the evening's sun glanced from a Moschino belt. At once the vendor stepped forward and, in the attitude of a traffic policeman, put up a hand to stop Steve.

"This way please ladies," he beamed, nodding graciously as one presented him deliberately with a pound coin. "Enjoy your meal." Then, looking down at Steve, the smile dissolved, upper lip slack against rounded gums. "What's wrong with the other side of the street? Go on, beat it."

Steve might have said something by way of a retort had it not been for his mobile, which had vibrated twice in his pocket. At the end of Temple Street he accessed the text message. It was from Martin. *"Come home at once,"* it read.

༄

"The police are holding Vinnie."

Steve could not immediately take this in: "What do you mean?"

"They've arrested him. He's being held in Manchester Airport."

"Oh no ..."

"Your mother's very upset."

In the silence that ensued they listened to Mary-Anne's voice rising and falling in the other room. She seemed to be crying and repeatedly blowing her nose.

"What happened?" Steve asked

"I'm afraid it's bad, Steve," Martin replied. "They caught him with a kilo of hash."

"Christ."

"He'll be looking at a stretch inside."

"Inside?"

"Prison, Steve. Vinnie's going to go to prison."

Steve found that he was crying. "How could he be so stupid?" he hoarsely whispered.

Martin moved to Steve's side and placed a hand on his shoulder. This was the first form of meaningful physical contact Steve had had with his stepfather in years. Rather than recoil from him he found himself moving towards the older man.

"What happened?" he asked again.

"He was on his way back from Amsterdam."

In his mind's eye Steve saw a sachet containing a lump of sticky black hash, this blistered beneath the opaque polythene.

"Your mother's making arrangements to see him tomorrow."

"Can I go?"

"Of course you can."

Steve moved to the window and looked down on the street outside. A young mother was strapping her toddler into a car seat, otherwise the place was deserted of people. Retraining his eyes, he brought Martin's reflection on the windowpane into focus. He seemed to be standing straighter and taller, his limbs newly invigorated, as if this disaster had distracted him from the crushing pressure of their predicament at Sycamore Drive. All the while, Mary-Anne was talking in the other room: she seemed to be repeating directions as if she were writing them at the same time. Her words sounded deeper, hollow. Steve turned: there was something in the tone of her words that wasn't quite right.

Martin watched as his stepson glanced from one corner of the room to the other. The impression was that "things" – books, folders, the radio etc. – had in some manner gravitated towards the door. It was as if someone had been clearing the room out. That was why your voice sounded empty, lacking warmth.

"They've found some tenants," Martin whispered by way of explanation.

"What do you mean?"

"There's a young family who want the house – as soon as they can get it."

"You're joking."

"Mary-Anne's talking about Monday week."

"But where are we going to live?" Steve stammered.

Now Martin's shoulders slackened into their defeated position. "The bookkeeper's sister at Tissons has a boarding house by the side of Melrose Park: *The Adriatic*."

"A boarding house? Melrose Park?"

"We're going to have the top floor."

SEVENTEEN

"Go forward please."

Having waited their turn in the queue for over ten minutes, Mary-Anne and Steve knew exactly what was expected of them. It was Mary-Anne who was first to take the four paces forward, and stop at the white line. The prison warder at the far end of the room then set off towards her, the dog, a longhaired Alsatian of black and tan, at her left heel. The dog looked uninterested, yet its nose was raised in the manner in which it had doubtless been trained. Mary-Anne was standing with her back to Steve. He saw her stiffen and tilt her head back a fraction, as if she were looking at the point at which the ceiling and walls met (there were no cornices here). He imagined that she probably had her eyes closed.

"Next."

Steve followed suit. As the dog rotated clockwise about his feet, he felt a muzzle stroke the back of his knee.

Now they must wait in an antechamber of sorts before being ushered through into the visiting room proper. There were two rectangular windows here, high up on the wall. A male warder, bearded and swarthy, sat behind a desk to one side of the door. Above him there was a poster, a picture of a top hat upside down on a table. Three tabby kittens were trying to climb from its chimney-like interior, ears pricked, eyes sparkling. It was the kind of poster you might buy in the open-air part of the market. Underneath, the caption read: *Some things in life are easier to get into than out of.*

"Go through now."

Ahead of them was a vast, low room, the size of an airport departure lounge. There were perhaps as many as fifty tables arranged symmetrically along its length, all with four chairs, one positioned at each corner. Mary-Anne and Steve went some paces forward, then stopped. The featureless drone of chatter filled their ears. To their left was a play area for children, with a post and rail fence of multicoloured plastic. Two toddlers were enacting a household scene within: pouring tea from a sky-blue teapot into cups and saucers of lemon yellow.

At last they saw Vinnie waving to them from a table halfway down the lounge.

"Oh, Vinnie," Mary-Anne breathed as she embraced her son. "Look at you; look at you ..."

But in actual fact, Steve thought, Vinnie did not look so different. Being a remand prisoner he was permitted to wear his own clothing – the clothing in which he had been apprehended. And his expression was not so altered. He had expected to find his brother deflated, depressed, unable to speak. If anything, his experiences of the past forty-eight hours had given Vinnie a new energy, a childlike vitality that Steve had not seen in years.

"Vinnie, what have you done?" Mary-Anne began.

"I haven't done anything. I've been stitched up."

But you could tell from Vinnie's expression, which was – and now Steve was definite – somehow alight with the novelty of his new predicament and plainly out of keeping with the surroundings, that this was not the truth.

"Oh: Vinnie."

"It was Erik. He put the stuff in my bag before I boarded."

"Vinnie, it's going to be so much easier for you if you tell the truth."

"It *is* the truth, Mum."

"What happened then?"

"We had the meeting with the mail order company – it went very well, no problems. We went for a meal out and then back to Erik's to collect my bag. We were running a bit late ... I just grabbed my case without thinking anything of it: I wouldn't have checked it anyway; why should I? I trusted him, you know. The bastard stitched me up."

"Vinnie! But are you *really* telling the truth?" Mary-Anne persisted.

Vinnie lowered his voice to a whisper. "If I wanted to buy a kilo of dope I could buy it without flying to Amsterdam," he intoned, his eyes ranging over the interior of the room.

Steve was convinced now that his brother was lying. He drew a deep, sad breath and surveyed the area before them, this time in the knowledge that this place would be Vinnie's home for the foreseeable future. There was an almost palpable air of resignation, defeat about the prison. Steve's gaze moved from table to table, each with its convicted prisoner (dressed in regulation clothing of loose hanging jeans, grey jersey, the neck edged in blue) and family seated like an audience about them. The prisoners had no common denominator: they were simply a cross-section of the men you might see on a busy pavement on any afternoon of the week: young, old, white, Chinese, African, Caribbean, Asian (this man had had to gather extra seats to receive his large family). What had they each done, Steve wondered, to end up here? And how would Vinnie hold his own in this company?

"I've brought you some clothes," Mary-Anne was saying.

"Oh, brilliant," Vinnie replied (again his choice of words betraying his guilt, Steve thought).

"And some food, some treats ..." Mary-Anne nodded, brushing away a tear.

"Come on, Mum," Vinnie frowned, feeling for his mother for the first time.

"What are we going to do?" she quietly cried.

"I'm seeing my solicitor tomorrow morning ..."

"With us ... moving out of Stanningley Terrace ..."

"What?" the other questioned, half straightening his posture.
"We're moving on Monday," Mary-Anne explained.
"Why?"
"Why do you think? We're bankrupt."
"Where are you going?"
"Melrose Park."
"Melrose Park?" Vinnie was blinking repeatedly, as if trying to erase the images of uncertainty that had doubtless swarmed into his mind. "What are you going to do with my room?" he then asked, and now there was an urgent tone to his voice. Steve could not help recalling his brother's nonchalant response of the afternoon when first their misfortunes had come to light. It was best to watch what you said in this world: the tables had a nasty habit of being turned against those who spoke their minds.

"We're storing everything in the attic: the family who are taking the house have agreed to let us do that. We can put a lock on the door."

Vinnie made no reply. He was visibly shaken; gone was his former ebullience. "I didn't realise," he muttered.

Steve was staring out of the windows of reinforced glass. The exchange between his older brother and Mary-Anne had in some manner drawn a line under their situation. Hearing it explained to another now made their move official. Life would be different from now on, it would be completely changed. Beyond the tall fences of wire netting, with their tangles of razor wire, the Vale of York stretched as far as the eye could see, green, flat, featureless, monotonous.

༜

Crash, crash.
"I'm coming in throwing punches ..."
Crash, crash.

"I'm coming through ... out of my way."

It was Martin, drunk. Steve moved to the landing at the top of the first flight of stairs, to watch his stepfather all but fall over the row of cardboard boxes that lined the hallway. It was a good job that Mary-Anne was out, fine-tuning arrangements at *The Adriatic*. From his position at the head of the stairs, Steve could have been a judge, staring down on a miscreant.

"Wanna see me win some cash? You're in for a treat."

"Martin!"

"Stand back, sir; the show is about to begin." And he withdrew a credit card from his back pocket.

Leaning heavily on the banisters, Martin pulled himself up to where Steve was standing. A strong smell of alcohol and cigar smoke clung to him, like an aura. The two briefly and silently acknowledged each other on the landing; then Martin was off, climbing the remaining two flights of stairs to Steve's bedroom. If Martin was thinking he was going to play the online casino for real, then he was mistaken: in order to do this you had to register your bank details – it would then take five days for casinocasino to open your e-cash account. For this reason Steve was in no hurry to follow his stepfather to the top floor. He was thinking instead of how best to sober him up before Mary-Anne's return. Martin had been in this kind of state before, the last time this Christmas gone by. What had they done then?

As Steve reached the doorway of his bedroom, Martin was waiting for Windows to load; he was also trying to read his bankcard by the light of the terminal.

"Martin, you can't just log on and play ..."

"What do you mean?"

"You have to register – they e-mail you with your account number and stuff."

"Registered days ago," was the simple answer, said with no emphasis.

Now it was Steve's turn to say: "What do you mean?"

"Got my account details, thank you very much. All I have to do now is give it a little infusion of electronic cash ..."

It was as if a chasm had opened up between the two, a crevasse of untold depth and danger.

"Oh no," Steve whispered.

Now Martin began to type, punching the number keypad with the index finger of his right hand. In this attitude he could have been a schoolmaster drilling home a point to a charge who had stepped out of line. The punching seemed to go on forever; then finally Martin sat back.

"Done it," he said; and then: "How much do I transfer? One thousand? Two thousand?"

"Martin: whose money is that?"

"It's the bank's money, stupid."

"Not Mum's money?"

"Since when did she give me any money?" he replied, unreasonably. "No, this money belongs to our flexible friend: if he thinks I'm good for three thousand then he *must* be right. Fifteen hundred then, yes ...?" And Martin deliberately punched the keys once more.

Steve may have won in the *"Practice Mode"*, but he sensed that his stepfather would lose playing the game for real. There was no question about it. "Martin don't, please," he implored the other.

But it was too late, for now Martin's face was bathed in the green glow of the baize before him.

"Right," he began, taking a deep breath through flared nostrils: "all on red, eh?"

Tick, tick, tick. From his position just inside the doorway (he had found himself edging into the room) Steve could not actually see the spinning roulette wheel. Now he craned a bit to his left.

"Twelve, red, even, player's a winner ..."

"Thankup ... And now all on black, yes?"

" Martin, don't ..."

Tick, tick, tick. This time Steve stepped into a position from which he could see the dancing ball. He blinked his eyes to produce the stroboscope effect.

"Twenty-two, black, even, player's a winner ..."

"This is too easy," Martin laughed. "What now? All on red?"

This time Steve raised his voice. "Martin don't ..."

There was a singsong quality to Martin's words now. "All on black then?"

"You're going to lose ..."

"Half on red, then," Martin compromised, and dragged three thousand pounds' worth of counters (these resembled lollipops, streaked and coloured, with £500 in blue against a background of gold) into the box containing the diamond of red.

"Four, black, even ..."

There was no announcement of "player's a loser" this time; just a *phut* as the counters were removed from the table, gone forever, vanished down the telephone wire.

"Hummpphh," Martin grunted. "Doesn't look as if it likes half measures. What now, then? All on red again."

"No," the other protested.

"Pick a number then?"

"No," Steve replied stubbornly.

There was a look of madness, not drunkenness, in Martin's eyes. "All on black then?"

Steve shook his head.

Martin turned to face his stepson square on. There was an imploring look in his eyes now; he gestured with both hands before him, palms rotated to the ceiling. "Steve, help me, please," he whispered. "You're good at this, you know how to get the numbers. If you don't help me, I'm just going to put this lot on black and we're going to lose. And we need to win."

Steve was checked by the use of the word "we". He frowned long and hard. Not for one second did Martin's penetrating gaze falter. "Please," Martin almost begged.

Steve stepped forward. At first he could not get the numbers to swim out of focus: it was akin to riding a bicycle or skating – you either "had" the technique or you didn't. Finally he managed to get the grid to distort. It was the number 20 that seemed to stand proud of the others.

"Twenty, then," he said.

"Twenty it is."

But Martin was not so foolish as to stake money "straight up". He placed five hundred pounds on the row 19, 20, 21.

Steve found himself holding his breath as the ball settled itself into its home.

"Nineteen, black, odd, player's a winner ..."

And written, top right: You have won £5,500.00 GBP.

"Yes," Martin whistled through his teeth, "that's my man, Steve. Yes!"

The two stared at one another with the kind of look you give someone who was once a good friend and who you are now meeting again for the first time in years.

"Another number," Martin then said, shaking himself free of this "embrace".

"No."

"Give me another number, man. Just a few more like that one and we'll be there."

Steve was staring at the words and numerals "Balance: £8,265.00", just below the *Spin* button. Martin was well ahead. He let the grid swim. "Seven," he breathed.

This time Martin did a corner bet, placing one thousand pounds on the intersection of the numbers 7, 8, 10 and 11. He also placed some counters of "his own" at the bottom end of the table, around the number 29. He even did one straight-up bet of two hundred pounds on 31. At thirty-five-to-one he would win seven thousand on this alone.

Tick, tick, tick.

"Six, black, even ..."

Martin did not appear to be put out by this. "Close," was all he said; then: "Another please."

Now Steve moved right up to the screen. He had all but predicted 6 for the last spin, but for some reason he had changed his selection to 7 at the very last moment: it was as if someone had been waving a red flag to distract him.

"Twenty-three," he now said.

Martin scattered the counters around the twenty three square, in trio bets, corner bets, streets, straight-up bets. By the time he had finished you could hardly read the numerals for chips in this second 12 portion of the table.

Tick, tick, tick.

"Eight, black, even ..."

Once again Martin was not put out. "Stand back, sir," he ordered Steve. "Come on: you're trying too hard; you're forcing it. Turn around."

Steve rotated clockwise on his feet. Looking blindly in the opposite direction, he resembled a tailor's dummy.

"Now choose a number," Martin said from behind him.

"But I can't see the table."

"Imagine it."

Steve could not do this: all he could see was the grid with the words *European Roulette* slanting left to right. There was no order to the numbers.

"Come on, we haven't got all night."

"Zero, then."

"You sure?"

"Martin ..."

"Zero it is."

Tick, tick, tick.

And then from Martin as the ball silenced itself: "Bloody hell!"
"What?"
"Zero, player's a winner ..."
Steve spun around to face the screen and to read the words "You have won £3,400.00 GBP".
"Get back, man," Martin growled, "and give me another number."
"Let's stop now."
"Another number, please."
"Seventeen."
This time there was just the *phut* as the counters were removed from the baize. There was the same outcome with the next spin, too. They were on a losing streak. Steve had to peer hard at the screen to read: "Balance: £3,890.00"
"Will you turn around?" Martin intoned. "In fact, get out; just give me the numbers from outside on the landing. Okay?"
Like a lamb, Steve obeyed and stood behind the closed door to his bedroom. There was a calmness here, quite in contrast to the sticky tension in front of the monitor. It was as if the light from the screen had the power to envelop you, to tether you like a dog on a leash.
"Come on," Martin sang from the other side of the door.
"This is mental ..."
"Come on, man ..."
"Eighteen then."
Since Steve could not hear the ticking of the ball, he could not keep abreast of the game. He just kept shouting out the numbers as they were demanded of him. After some minutes, during which time, Steve imagined, there must have been quite a number of spins, he heard the chair scrape over the floor as his stepfather stood from his position in front of the computer. Had everything been lost?
But Martin's expression told a different story. His face seemed to be bathed in a golden glow: it was as if every muscle had softened

into a bed of feathers.

"You're the bloody Shining, you are," he gasped for the second time that month, grasping Steve's hand.

"What do you mean?"

"We're eighty thousand up: that's what I mean."

"You're joking."

"See for yourself."

Steve followed him to the terminal to read: "Balance: £82,540.00".

"That's amazing," he breathed. "We're finished, yeah?"

"Finished, my arse."

"Martin: you've won eighty thousand pounds."

"And I need a hundred and thirty."

There was a second long silence between the two. Having met each other for the first time in years, they were now weighing one another up, it would appear, since this time there was a wariness in their penetrating gazes. Steve's eyes travelled to the floor, where the telephone wire from the modem was plugged into its BT box. But Martin was ahead of him here. As his stepson ducked to floor level to wrench the wire from its socket, the older man was on to him, and grasped one wrist with a hold of iron.

"Don't even think about it ..."

"Martin, you're hurting me ..."

"So give me a number ..."

"Please let go of my hand ..."

With a deliberate shake of the head, as if he had surfaced from a dive and was shaking the water from his hair and ears, Martin relinquished his hold on his stepson's hand. This he did slowly and carefully, ready to grasp him once more should the necessity arise. Indeed he shuffled his foot one step to the right: he had the BT socket covered. When he spoke, it was with quite a different voice: he had returned to his senses, it seemed.

"Steve, we need to do one more bet," he said calmly.

"Martin, I can't help you."

"Eighty thousand is a lot of money, but it's not enough. If we don't get what we need then we may as well have nothing."

Again the use of the word "we" checked Steve, yet this time he would not compromise.

"Martin, I can't help you," he repeated.

"So you're not with me any more?"

"I can't help you," was the firm reply.

"So be it," Martin said with an air of grimness, sitting before the terminal once again.

Now Steve could have darted to the skirting board and ripped the wire from the wall, but something held him back. Perhaps Martin would win on this last bet; perhaps if he lost then that was what was "meant". Whatever his reasoning (and even he did not know), he stood passively by.

"All on red then," Martin whispered, this said with a note of exhaustion or resignation. "Or all on black?"

Steve was silent.

"Red or black. Fifty bloody fifty. Red or black."

Still Martin could not shift the counters onto a square; he seemed paralysed by indecision. He turned momentarily from the screen, as if seeking inspiration. On Steve's bed there was a counterpane of black and white squares; on the floor, by the side of the bed, there was a small durrie, streaked red. Martin whipped back to the computer.

"Red," he spat.

It took some time to drag all the chips onto the red diamond. Finally the eighty thousand was staked. The cursor hovered over the *Spin* button – then, with a click, the wheel was activated.

Tick, tick, tick.

Steve had to look away: it was as if he were awaiting the report from an artillery cannon, awaiting the shock waves and concussion.

Tick, tick, tick.

Martin resembled a waxwork figure, arrested in time, his breath clamped in his chest.

"Twenty-eight, black, even ..."

Neither said a word.

With a *phut* the counters dissolved, vanished from their position on the red diamond. It was a *phut* no louder than any other *phuts*. And now the balance line read "Balance: £00.00". It would have been better if a croupier had raked away the multicoloured counters: that way, hearing them touching one another as they slid over the baize to form an irregular pile ready for sorting, you would understand better that you had lost: this way your money just vanished down the telephone wire. "Balance: £00.00"

Martin slumped forwards, his forehead hitting the keyboard. "Oh, no," he groaned.

Steve stared stupidly at the screen. Martin had hit a number of different keys as he had crashed forwards. This had activated a message from casinocasino: *"Are you sure you want to exit from the Casino?"* it read.

EIGHTEEN

"If it's busy, I wait at the corner at the bottom of the street," Mrs Ariadne was explaining. "Then when the coast is clear I go in. I say *Phit-Pet* (a dog-walking service operated by her niece) have ten dogs today. And the butcher – he's a very big man – he take out a great, how you call it, 'handful' of bits – very good bits – out of a plastic dustbin. One handful is fifty-pence; two handful one-pound. Is very good value. Is nothing wrong with it. Is completely fresh."

Steve was pushing at the pieces of meat with his fork, as if trying to submerge them in the soup; but they kept rising to the surface. Now that Mrs Ariadne had revealed the provenance of her ingredients, he fancied he could see the indigo ink on a piece of skin, the type of ink that had once read *New Zealand* on the haunch of a spring lamb.

"It's very good, Mrs Ariadne," Mary-Anne said, "a bit like a cassoulet."

Under virtually any other circumstances Martin would have muttered "cassoowhat" or "cassoulet, my arse"; but today he was silent. Since they had arrived at *The Adriatic* he had hardly spoken a word.

"My sister very good cook," Mrs Ariadne went on, pouring herself a glass of water from the type of jug you might find in a school. "She come and work at the embassy, you know – long time ago."

"The embassy?" Mary-Anne politely enquired.

"Yes, the embassy. The big building in London. She very good cook. I learn everything from her."

They could either eat with Mrs Ariadne and the other guests in the hotel – at present one permanent, (Mona Campbell in Room 9), and two backpackers – in which case they should give Mrs Ariadne notice that morning, or they could prepare their own meal in a small kitchenette on the mezzanine floor. For whatever reason – probably out of politeness – Mary-Anne had opted for a meal with their hostess. A "three-course dinner" here – fruit juice, casserole and ice-cream – would cost three pounds each each. Not bad value, Mary-Anne had commented.

Now Mrs Ariadne was gesturing at Martin, speaking over him, as it were.

"Your husband: he a builder? Maybe he do me some jobs."

Steve saw his stepfather flinch, as if he had been given a very weak electric shock.

"My husband is having a break from work," Mary-Anne answered.

"He not looking well, are you, Mr Lenton? He on disability pay?"

"He's just having a break, that's all," Mary-Anne said, firmer.

Steve was not worried for Martin (in spite of the fact he had heard his mother say to him, "Now don't go and do anything silly, will you?" – this heard through the paper-thin walls of their attic rooms); but now his heart went out to him. There had been a distinct absence of recrimination as they had packed up their belongings in Stanningley Terrace. What had happened had happened, apparently: it was to be viewed as a fact of life, something that now had to be coped with. But there was artificiality about this. It was as if Mary-Anne had managed to freeze her feelings, arrest their movement. Perhaps if they had been harder on Martin he would not have been so hard on himself. But he looked so forlorn as he sat there, automatically spooning his soup; he was a shadow of his former self. You could not help but feel for him at least.

"Maybe one night you come to Bingo," Mrs Ariadne was saying. "Last week the snowball was two hundred and forty thousand pound."

"I had no idea you could win so much," Mary-Anne politely answered once again, although now you could tell that she was losing patience.

"Is wired nationally. If they losing in Dorset, we winning in Yorkshire ..."

"Well, we don't gamble, Mrs Ariadne – do we?"

"Maybe is good thing: gambling can make you crazy, like drink."

"We don't drink either," Mary-Anne flatly stated.

"You very sensible family. Is a tragedy shame you are homeless."

"We're not homeless ... we're just between houses."

"My sister, she say you were on street."

Here Martin stood, the chair legs scraping against the linoleum floor. There was a wild look in his eyes. As he fled to the door, Mary-Anne rose to follow.

"I open my big mouth, eh?" Mrs Ariadne asked of Steve.

Steve smiled wanly and shrugged.

"You want ice-cream now?"

"Yes, please."

"If your father not coming back I give you a double portion."

Although *The Adriatic* was quite a substantial building, there was a distinct lack of privacy here. The door to Mrs Ariadne's sitting room seemed to be permanently open, a murmur from the television always audible, the flickering of the screen at night throwing shadows across the hallway. She was the kind of person who would make an ideal witness for the police: she would know to the minute the movements of each of her guests, and so be in a position to support or discount alibis with one of her matter-of-fact shrugs of the shoulders. The first night they had spent here Steve had become disorientated and, at about four o'clock in the morning, had found himself on the landing outside his room. The stairwell was dark save for the thin green light of the bulb that illuminated the sign

Fire Exit. Mrs Ariadne must have been asleep in a chair.

"You okay? You want your Mummy?" she had called up to the top floor.

"I'm just going to the bathroom," Steve answered.

"Don't flushing toilet, please: pipes make bad knock."

They had only seen Mona Campbell twice since the weekend. At first Mary-Anne had viewed her with suspicion, as if she might be a working girl. But it turned out she was a specialist nurse from Aberdeen, much sought-after by the school of medicine in which she was trained (acute orthopaedics) due to chronic shortages in staffing. She worked long, regular hours, but you could tell when she was in her room as she left her shoes neatly outside the door. There was evidence of her in the bathroom too – a blue toothbrush and a pink flannel – otherwise there was not much to go on.

Mary-Anne had negotiated an all-in rate of one hundred and thirty pounds per week for the two attic rooms. This was for a minimum period of six months, in keeping with the short-term tenancy agreement they had signed with the young family who had been so eager to take Stanningley Terrace. Rental income from this was one thousand, two hundred and fifty pounds per calendar month. In terms of their day to day expenses – with savings on energy bills, council tax, household insurance etc. – they were at least the right side of the line. Once the deal had been forged, Mary-Anne's mood was transformed.

"Just take what you really need," she had said, and they could have been packing for a holiday.

But the following morning, just hours before the move, Steve had studied his mother from an upstairs window as she checked the bird-boxes in the garden. These were so positioned as to allow observation from her work desk in the back sitting room. It was her greatest joy to watch the development of the families of tits – one year there had been a brood of wrens – as the fledglings made their first tentative efforts at flight, and as, somehow, incredibly, they managed, each and every one of them, to return to the safety of their crowded boxes. This was the only time Steve saw the ice thaw. And of course it begged the question in its most distilled form: would they be back in Stanningley Terrace to witness the arrival of the new generation of birds the following spring? In fact, would they ever be back?

It would take time to really understand how you felt about an event of this magnitude. You would need to sleep, wake up, sleep again: perhaps as many as a dozen times for the real essence of the situation to reveal itself to you. That first afternoon, for instance, encouraged by Mary-Anne's example no doubt, Steve had been able to view the move as a new beginning of sorts: not exactly a holiday, but as a trip away from home. Yet only hours later he had been overtaken by a crushing depression. His attic – the smaller of the two – was at the back of the building, and the Velux window that gave onto Melrose Park offered a view of a gentle slope of grass, a stand of beech trees to the right. It would have been better if he had been street-side. The park was so grim, so dark. At the top of the slope there was a children's play area. Silhouetted against the evening twilight, a number of youths were perched, like a colony of primates, on a climbing frame. Steve had watched them assemble, throwing their bikes to the ground, climbing into their hierarchical positions. He was no snob, but this was no company for him: these kids were rough. Indeed a figure was walking at this very moment from left to right towards the play area; in both hands he held a leash, his arms before him in the attitude of a somnambulist as he restrained two Staffordshire bull terriers. To cross the park, a shortcut to the bus stop for school, would be like walking the plank. He would have to rise fifteen minutes early each morning.

And then there was the sound of traffic, or rather the lack of it. No matter how still you stood, how carefully you listened, you could not hear the motorway from here. Sometimes the drum of the city might suggest the lanes of tarmac, so too the resonance of aircraft (they must be under a flight-path on Melrose Park), but in reality the M62 was some miles off. It had at first made Steve feel vulnerable and unprotected. But once he had confronted these agents of loneliness he had felt, if anything, stronger. Beyond that, his probing about the carnation in the glass jar had served to shield him further – but perhaps for the wrong reasons.

"Have you been, do you ever go to the cemetery?" he asked of his mother that night as she sat at the end of his bed (something she had not done in six years).

"I never go," Mary-Anne had answered.

"You don't mind if I go?" Steve queried.

"Why should I mind, darling? In fact, your going there makes me ..." Her words had tailed off.

Steve had been on the point of describing the flower he had discovered beneath his father's headstone; but he held back. If it hadn't been Mary-Anne who had tenderly placed the white bloom against the short-cropped grass, then who could it have been? Martin? Out of guilt? The same guilt that had drawn Steve there, like a magnet? Most unlikely. Was it possible then that his father had had a mistress? Were there others who loved him? For an instant the blood had burnt in his veins.

He pushed away from the window and sat on his bed. You had to be careful not crack your head on the ceiling here, as the divan was tucked tight beneath the eaves. His eyes settled on the plastic tray to the right of the window, with its baby kettle and saucer of tea bags and sachets of powdered milk and sugar. A blackness began to settle about him. He tried to rally his thoughts by focusing on Mrs Holland's words of advice. But this only produced a snort of impatience. It was all very well to lie there, dispensing pearls of wisdom from the comfort of your bed. Didn't she realise that you would need to be seated in a hostel like this, with its threadbare rug, its bedside-side table, the veneer splintered and missing in places, staring at your future as if down the barrel of a rifle, to know what it was *really* like? If only there were an *Undo* icon now! One click of the mouse after another and you could backtrack to the point at which you took the wrong turning.

An image of a maze suggested itself to Steve. Some years before, on a weekend away north of Alnwick in Northumberland, he and Mary-Anne had spent some hours in a labyrinth of sugar beet cut by an enterprising farmer. Steve had gone on ahead, inspired by the novelty of their situation. The sun bore down on him above the tunnel of poisonous green, the felled beet dank underfoot. It was both hot and cold in those metres of right-angled corridors. He had crashed ahead, determined to break free from his mother, completely and utterly. Only, right in the middle of this maze he had disturbed a couple in their lovemaking. The man had turned to give Steve such a look of hatred, the kind of look you can never forget. Given his exuberance, the effect was devastating. *The Adriatic* had that same capability. Blows of this nature had the effect of making you grow up. They seemed to trip you into the future.

NINETEEN

"I'm going to be a master builder, me. Not just any old chippy, and not one of them builders you see on sites – but a craftsman, a master builder. I'm going to work on houses footballers and rock stars have bought."

"But today you're a *Big Issue* salesman," Steve retorted.

Buzz was not irked by this. "Steve, this is a means to an end," he grinned. "You can't just snap your finger, you know."

"You're stopping at school, then?" (There had been some talk of Buzz not sitting his GCSEs.)

"English and Maths; that's all I need. They're holding a place for me in September."

They had had to walk some distance to reach this position, one hundred metres beyond the bus terminus, as most of the patches were keenly guarded. There appeared to be a clearly defined pecking order. You couldn't just stand in front of San Petino, for instance, even if you did have some magazines to sell. You would have to inherit this site, or have an arrangement (probably involving payment) with the vendor to look after his area when he was off duty.

What was remarkable was how close to the street you came, close to the general detritus and flotsam of mankind. The sidewalks and gutters were like beaches: discarded objects would turn up, as if deposited there by an ebbing tide. Steve had seen a broken umbrella projecting from a dustbin, whole vases of flowers against the kerb, books, and, most peculiarly of all, a complete manicure set. In just a few days, like many of the other vendors, Buzz had adopted the attitude of a beachcomber, zigzagging from one bin to another.

He had yet to take more than a passing interest in their contents, though, just exclaiming "Will you look at that!" if the wire basket within the pebbledash pedestals held anything unusual.

Buzz was quite unabashed in his quest for sales, and could approach the public with complete confidence: *"Big Issue, sir? Big Issue, madam? Do you have this week's edition? Would you like any assistance, madam?"* There were some people who were more likely to give to charity than others, and from his customary position of fifteen paces off, Steve would fall into a routine of betting against himself who would stop to reach for their purses and who would not. When you got it right a few times in a row it was like a yankee coming off ...

It was strange, but over the past fortnight Steve had spent more time with Buzz than ever before. The nights would be drawing in presently, like great curtains, and he knew he must make as much as possible of these hours of daylight, since evenings at *The Adriatic* would soon be interminable, one long tunnel from when you got in after school till when you must once again emerge the following morning, darkness about your shoulders. The prospect was daunting. But he had also wanted to keep an eye on Buzz. It was common knowledge that the drug scene had lately taken root on the streets, some of the vendors openly dealing fiver-bags of *brown* and *stones* to support their habits. Buzz seemed to have no interest in this, however. There was money to be made here, that went without saying, but he was shrewd enough to understand that most of the dealers became, as he put it, *their own best customers.*

"We'll take a walk," he said, joining Steve at his position within a doorway.

Together they crossed the road opposite the bus station, making way for the crowds of people who milled about, like termites at the head of their nest.

"Twenty-three quid since two thirty," Buzz mused. "You ought to get some copies, Steve."

"I haven't got your touch ..."

"Nothing ventured, nothing gained."

They came to a halt before a branch of a building society (not the building society that had lent money on Stanningley Terrace, Steve silently noted). Beyond the glass pane, positioned on a shelf of blue velvet, someone had arranged a number of square, plastic money boxes, these built up like building blocks. To one side a poster detailed a particular type of savings account. On the other side a different poster advertised life assurance and read: *Cash if you die, cash if you don't.* Ordinarily this slogan would have provoked a remark from one or both of the boys, or at least a grunt. Today they were silent. What could you say?

In the reflection of the glass Steve saw a procession of vehicles, headed by a black Bentley, pass slowly from left to right, travelling towards the city centre. The Bentley sported a small flag over its bonnet of Whitby jet.

"Ey up: Lord Mayor," Buzz murmured.

"What's going on there?"

"Maybe some kind of demo ..."

"Coming?"

"I'll stop here," Buzz answered, stepping away from the bank with his bundle of magazines, these held like a cocktail tray, as he approached a party of Japanese tourists.

The motorcade was snaking left and out of view into Coverdale Street, the indicators of the half a dozen vehicles flashing gold. Steve pushed away from the glass pane and followed. Before turning in the wake of the Bentley he glanced back at Buzz, who was now deep in conversation with the tourists, pointing this way, showing them that way. These directions would cost, Steve thought with a grin.

It turned out that there were as many as two hundred people gathered before a building halfway down Coverdale Street. These termites were packed closer together than those in front of the bus terminus. A faint resonance of voices filled the void between the tall, soulless buildings typical of the area (this was the insurance and banking sector, only this part of it was devoid of restaurants, bars, shops even). The Lord Mayor must have been running late, as, judging by his position before an entrance of glass and stainless steel, he was already preparing to speak. The Lady Mayoress was there, too, as well as one other assistant. As the mayor chatted briefly with a pinstripe-suited man, his two helpers were checking over a small amplifier, to which was attached a microphone. Steve quickened his step. He was just approaching the periphery of the crowd when the mayor began.

"Good afternoon, ladies and gentlemen. It gives me great pleasure as a representative of the City Council to be here today, to celebrate what I can only describe as a truly remarkable occasion. There are defining moments in time, when you feel there has come a punctuation mark, if you like. Well, I think we have started a new paragraph." Pause. "But if some of you feel this is the start of a new chapter, well, I don't think I can blame you: I think you may well be right."

He paused again. The crowd seemed to edge nearer. Steve pressed closer. It was hard to catch all the mayor's words over the general thunder of traffic.

"Now, I am told by reliable sources that these solar panels could make two thousand pieces of toast each and every day ... even if the sun wasn't shining ... and we all know quite a lot about that ..."

Laughter. As the mayor waved a hand aloft, so most people glanced skywards, chins raised, as if they were at an air show. Steve was quick to follow suit. He saw that the top floor of this new building was not a glass-fronted office, like the others in the street, rather it was clad in a deep, glossy blue, its surface being made up of a series of silver edged panels. These were solar panels, or, more precisely, photovoltaic cells.

"A truly incredible fact. And there are many, many more extraordinary and of course more meaningful statistics ... For instance, we know that solar generated power could provide *ten thousand times* (said with deliberate incredulity) more energy than the world currently uses ... and that if we covered just a small fraction of the Sahara desert with PV cells we could generate all the world's electricity requirements."

More nodding. Briefly Steve pictured a corner of the desert draped in blue, like wax on a tablecloth: it made an incongruous image.

"These are the first panels" – another turn of the wrist – "you will find in any city centre throughout the UK. It therefore fills me with a sense of great pride to know that it was a company in this town has been the first to make that bold, decisive step. Once more we are pioneers: pioneers of a new age. Others will be following our example, if only for commercial reasons, since not only will these panels provide free, clean electricity to service the building, I am told that any surplus energy – energy generated over the weekend, for example – will be sold to the national grid."

Steve was still staring at the panels, their surfaces reflecting the sky beyond. An aeroplane was passing east, towards Leeds and Bradford airport, its flight-path kinked as it leapt from one panel to another. Eventually he lowered his gaze, to glance in the direction of the mayor once more. And started. For there was a familiar face in the crowd beyond the doorway. There was no point in pretending he hadn't noticed that person, for his eyes had already locked a second too long. It was Robin Fellowes. Steve smiled over the sea of heads that separated them, but his smile was wafer-thin. He must keep up the pretence, however, for now there were two pairs of eyes on him. The other pair belonged to Helena.

The mayor was tugging at a rope of satin. Everyone craned to see what would happen next. Steve's view of Robin and Helena was obstructed, and anyway, in a show of casual indifference he, too, turned to watch the mayor. A final tug of the rope brought a piece of cloth to the pavement, to reveal a simple plaque and an electricity meter, this perhaps ten inches in diameter. A hand on the meter-face was pointing to four o'clock. There was clapping and cheering.

Over the applause Steve looked back in the direction of Robin and Helena. Helena was wearing an anorak of mauve, its hood edged with artificial fur. Her hair was tied in one bunch and, unusually, she was wearing spectacles. For this reason, with her expression fixed in a measured scrutiny, she looked older, more mature. Robin was smiling broadly as he clapped, his small ponytail trembling at the back of his neck. He seemed to be standing too close behind her, that or she had positioned herself too close in front of him. Both of them continued to beam in the direction of the mayor, allowing Steve the opportunity of scrutinising them further. Robin seemed to be chewing gum. The top of Helena's head was almost below his chin.

Of course, Robin and Helena were a couple! Steve tried to avert his eyes. But it was too late. It was as if he had been caught by a crashing wave as he walked innocently on a boulevard before the ocean. A sense of bitterness and longing had drenched him and now seemed to pervade each and every cell in his body. Helena and Robin Fellowes an item! How could it be? He continued to stare at the pavement, consciously amazed by the strength of feeling that had risen, silent like a serpent from the undergrowth, to constrict his throat, his very being. He had lost Anita, he had lost on the horses, he had lost his life in Stanningley Terrace, he had lost his brother, he had lost his father, even – but none of these, it seemed, could compare with the loss of Helena, could compare with the loss of this person to another person.

"Thank you, ladies and gentlemen, for helping me to celebrate this unique occasion. The show of support here is testimony to the determination of this generation to discover and harness new, clean and efficient forms of energy ..."

Steve could turn and walk away, yet he must confront Helena, he must torture himself with the truth, it seemed. As the crowds began to dissolve around him, he made his way over to where they were both standing, apparently waiting to speak to the man in the pinstripe suit. Helena had not been at school yet that term; she had recently suffered the loss of her father (Steve had learnt this from her friend, Samantha). Indeed her hair was tied in a black bow.

"Hi."

"Hi."

"I'm sorry ... about your dad."

"Thank you."

Robin Fellowes turned to join them. "If it isn't the snake expert," he said, not unkindly.

"Hi, Robin."

Robin placed his arm around Helena's shoulders, his fingers a scrubbed pink over the folds of blue. "I always knew he was our side of the fence," he said, addressing Helena.

Helena laughed her warm, half-sceptical laugh. Her teeth flashed white and moist.

Some minutes of small talk followed. Helena had returned to work as a volunteer at *The Pennine Recycling Plant* over the holidays, it transpired. All the records had got into a "hopeless tangle" on the computer system: she had improved efficiency no end, it seemed. Finally, Robin Fellowes turned in the direction of the mayor.

A moment of silence passed before Steve stammered: "You're not ..."

"Not what?" Helena asked, at once alive to the preposterous notion that had seeded itself in the other's mind.

"You're not ... going out with Robin, are you?"

Helena would not reply at first. Now there was an expression of sympathy in her eyes. "What are you like?" she eventually murmured.

A sensation of warm relief reached across Steve's chest. He could not help but smile.

"When are you coming back to school?" he then asked.

"I'm not."

"What do you mean?"

Again there was a look of sympathy, dismay even, in Helena's eyes. "We're moving," she answered. "We're going to live with my Nan."

"Going to live with your Nan?"

"In Fife."

" ... Why?"

"My Mum's not taken it well, my Dad dying and that."

Once more Steve must proceed as if in the dark. "Helena, I'm really sorry," he stated selfishly.

Helena paused before responding. "I'm sorry too ..."

"I'll miss you," Steve managed.

Helena would not reply to this – she just flashed a smile.

On his way out of Coverdale Street, Steve turned one last time to survey the scene he had just left. The crowds had more or less dissolved; the mayor had long gone to attend to another appointment; just a few knots of people remained. The office building stood like one-eyed Cyclops, staring fixedly into the autumn afternoon. Robin and Helena were by now at the other end of the street, just about to pass out of view. A skein of geese, a giant V, was moving high and silent in the cloudless sky, just south of the city. Its passage was so impressive it almost had the power to take you with it.

꙰

A Note About the Author

Matthew Yorke was born in London and now works in Leeds as an engineer. He is author of *The March Fence*, for which he won the John Llewellyn Rhys Prize, and editor of *Surviving: The Uncollected Works of Henry Green.*

Praise for *The March Fence*

"This is a novel which throbs with life and wonder at the manifold varieies of experience ... The talent for writing novels may be hard to define, yet it is unmistakable when encountered ... [*The March Fence*] is the real thing ... the best first novel that I have read in a long time." – Allan Massie, *The Scotsman*

"A most impressive debut."
– Elaine Feinstein, *The Times*

"Distinctive, energetic ... the narrative takes a real grip ..."
– Hilary Mantel, *Daily Telegraph*

"[P]recision and craftsmanship ... form the ... backbone of this thoughtful and unusual [first] novel.
– Leslie Dick, *New Statesman*

OTHER BOOKS FROM

WAYWISER

Poetry

Al Alvarez, *New & Selected Poems*
Peter Dale, *One Another*
B.H. Fairchild, *The Art of the Lathe*
Joseph Harrison, *Someone Else's Name*
Anthony Hecht, *Collected Later Poems*
Anthony Hecht, *The Darkness and the Light*
Timothy Murphy, *Very Far North*
Daniel Rifenburgh, *Advent*
Mark Strand, *Blizzard of One**
Deborah Warren, *The Size of Happiness*
Clive Watkins, *Jigsaw*
Richard Wilbur, *Mayflies**
Richard Wilbur, *Collected Poems 1943-2004*
Norman Williams, *One Unblinking Eye*

Non-Fiction

Neil Berry, *Articles of Faith: The Story of British Intellectual Journalism*
Mark Ford, *A Driftwood Altar: Essays and Reviews*
Richard Wollheim, *Germs: A Memoir of Childhood*

*Expanded UK edition